Finding Charlie

by

Jerri Drennen

Men and Women of Valor

Finding Charlie

Cover Art by *The Wild Rose Press, Inc.*

The Wild Rose Press, Inc.
PO Box 708
Adams Basin, NY 14410-0708
Visit us at www.thewildrosepress.com

Publishing History
First Edition, 2026
Trade Paperback Print ISBN 978-1-5092-6464-3
Digital ISBN 978-1-5092-6465-0

Men and Women of Valor
Published in the United States of America

Dedication

This book is dedicated to my Army son, Nathan, who helped me with any military questions I had.

Chapter 1

Bryan Gamble sat in a chair outside his boss, Vince Samuels' office, his ass almost going numb. Over an hour had passed since he'd been summoned to Bolton's Valor Security and Investigations, and the idleness was starting to wear on him.

"I'm sorry for the long wait," his assistant, Nina Alverez, said, shuffling a stack of papers on her desk. "Vince thought he'd be ready for you by now. I guess he misjudged how long his meeting would run."

"Is it true Congressman Reed's daughter is missing?" Dennis Reed was the representative from the company's district here in Winding Creek, Colorado, and had helped a time or two with finding funding for the group to stay afloat—no worries now, since they had more clients than they could handle.

"That's what we've been told. I don't have specifics. I imagine that's what they're discussing. You'll have to wait and speak with Vince."

Bryan shifted, trying to reposition himself on the seat. He'd be lucky to be able to stand if he had to sit here much longer, reminding him of those overseas trips spent on cargo planes for hours on end. This was hard for him. Staying in one place for any length of time taxed his mental state. ADHD did that to a person, a disorder he was diagnosed with in his early teens. Not a bad thing for a soldier of war, which he was up until six months ago, but for this, not so good. At that moment, all he wanted to do was get up and leave.

Just then, the adjoining room door opened, and the congressmen and Vince stepped out, both men looking grim. This wasn't good. From their expressions, whatever had happened to Reed's daughter was a life-or-death situation. If they didn't locate her soon, she'd probably be found dead.

"Bryan, this is Congressman Reed. Dennis, this is Bryan Gamble, our tracker. If anyone can find Charlie, it's him."

Bryan stuck out his hand, nervous to be put in such an important role. Yes, he could track a combative in a foreign country, but this was totally different. This was American soil where rules applied, and he'd only been with Valor for three short months. Up until today, he'd watched as the team investigated cases. To be chosen to find this missing woman made every nerve in his body charge, and not necessarily in a good way.

Was Vince sure Bryan could handle taking lead on a case?

The congressman grasped his hand with both of his and held tight to his fingers like they were a lifeline.

Bryan cleared his throat and glanced at Vince.

"Dennis has filled me in on his daughter's comings and goings. All her friends and work colleagues. I'll have all of it for you to take so we can get started. No ransom demands have been made, so you know the more time that passes, the less chance we have of a good outcome. So, we need to get moving pronto. I gave Sterling a heads-up. He's going to be your tech support. Anything you need, no matter what it is, he'll be there to help with info and locations on any of her contacts."

"Please find my daughter," the congressman said, his deep blue eyes now glassy in appearance. "She is all I have."

Byran's gut clenched. He had to find her.

"I'll keep you in the loop, Dennis. If we learn anything, you'll be the first to know." Vince led the man out of the office. When he returned, he sighed. "I can't tell you how important finding Charlie alive is, Bryan. None of the media outlets know that she's missing. Let's keep it that way."

"Yes, sir."

"Let me get that information and you can get started."

Bryan waited by the door, thinking he'd check out her work first, see when she was last seen. That would give him a timeline on when she'd disappeared and who could have possibly taken her.

Vince stepped out and handed him what looked like four or five sheets of paper and a manila envelope. This was going to take longer than he thought. How many friends and work associates did the woman have?

Vince slapped him on the back. "I know this is your first assignment, Bryan, but I know how capable you are. I trust you to find her alive. Inside the envelope is a recent picture of Charlie and a set of keys to her apartment in case you need access."

"Okay. I will do everything I can to find her, Captain. The congressman deserves no less than us saving his daughter."

"Call me if you learn anything important. Now, go find Charlie."

Bryan took off for the elevators, skimming through the sheets his boss had given him. He spotted a name that stood out, causing the hairs on the back of his neck to stand up. Sanderson Emery. A billionaire entrepreneur who was a womanizer in the worst sense of the word. Why did the congressman's daughter know him? Did they travel in the same circles? He read through the entry, and his jaw dropped. Charlene Elizabeth Reed was dating the man? No accounting for taste, that was for sure. Yet, this just put him on the top of the list of suspects in her disappearance, and he'd be the first Bryan would interview since his initial reaction was a bit of a sixth-sense gift of his. He only hoped Emery would be willing to meet with him.

He took out his phone and called Sterling. The man picked up on the second ring. "What do you need?"

"Can you find out where Sanderson Emery is at this moment?"

"Sure thing. Give me five minutes and I'll call you back."

Bryan exited the elevator on the first floor of the Hyland building and walked to the front entrance. Bolton's Valor S&I was on the fifteenth, a fact that he'd been surprised by when he had first come in for his interview. Only well-established companies had offices on that floor, and Valor was a start-up. Clearly, Vince knew people in high places. Then again, they were looking for a congressman's daughter, and you couldn't get much higher than that on the food chain.

****

Charlie's heart raced. In the pitch-black darkness, she could barely make out the walls around her. The floor was ice cold, rough to the touch. Some type of concrete by the way it felt. How had she gotten here? Why couldn't she remember? Last thing she could recall was leaving the Oasis Club after meeting a friend for a few drinks. Someone must have been following her and then everything was a blank.

She took a labored breath, never having been this scared in her life. Why was she there? What were they going to do to her? All these horrible scenarios took shape in her mind, especially after having seen every *Saw* movie ever made. Were they going to cause her enormous pain before they killed her? Who were they, and why had they taken her?

Charlie started to shake. She had to do something, but what?

She sat on the floor, her hands tied behind her back, her feet secured in front of her. She could barely move and sat thinking about what they could do to her. She had to think. Calm down and use her brain. There had to be a way to get out of there. After all, she had a black belt and had hand-to-hand combat training, hardly some damsel in distress. Somehow, she needed to use that knowledge to free herself.

Maybe she could at least get her hands in front of her if she scooted them under her butt and legs. It was going to be a struggle, but it was better than sitting here waiting to die.

Loud, male voices from beyond the room stopped her in her tracks. Was it too late? Were they coming to murder her now?

Bile worked its way up her dry throat, her stomach forcing those drinks she'd had that night to come up.

She leaned to the side and heaved, only expelling a bit of acidy liquid.

The door creaked and she sat straight up as bright light filtered into the room, blinding her.

When she could make out a figure, the person standing there wore some kind of grotesque mask, only frightening her more. Her lips started to quiver, tears threatening to fall, but she refused to allow that.

"Who are you and what are you going to do to me?" she asked, her voice trembling.

"You'll know soon enough," the man shot back, then laughed. "I'm going to untie your hands and feet so you can eat and go to the bathroom if you need to. There is a bucket in the corner for that. I know you are used to the finer things in life, but you aren't getting that here. If you're lucky and your father comes through, you'll get out of here alive. That is, if you don't give me any trouble. Do you understand?"

When she didn't answer, he stepped over and kicked her hard in the calf. "Do you understand?"

"Yes," she said, pain radiating up her leg. Clearly, this guy didn't care that she was a woman and he'd have no qualms to beating her within an inch of her life if she tried to escape. But would he kill her anyway? That was a possibility and a reason for her to at least attempt to find a way out given the chance.

He walked over and quickly clipped the restraints, then left for a moment and returned with a tray that held a small lantern type light, food, and a roll of toilet paper.

"Enjoy your meal. It may just be your last if Daddy decides you aren't worth our price."

Chapter 2

Bryan almost snapped when Sanderson's assistant told him the man wasn't there. The ping on his cell phone said he was here at the office, which meant this asshole was lying to him. But what could he do about it? Maybe storm through the door and prove the man was indeed there, but would that gain Emery's cooperation? Probably not, and it could get Bryan arrested. That, he didn't need.

"I'm going to leave you my card. If you could have him call me when he's available, I would appreciate it. Let him know it's about his girlfriend." Bryan was going to kill the man with kindness and hope it would help get his boss to call him today. Time was of the essence. Every hour that passed meant more uncertainty of Charlie being found alive.

Bryan turned to leave. Next on the list was all the people Charlie worked with at her non-profit organization, Starting Over. On the notes he'd been given, it revealed the place helped battered women find jobs to support themselves and their children without the help of their abusive husbands. A worthy cause for sure.

Charlie had worked there for over three years now, and Bryan was going to have to talk to everyone she interacted with on a daily basis. Could one of those abusive husbands have taken her? That could be a possibility if they thought Charlie had helped separate them from their families. And this just made his list potentially longer.

First things first. Find out who saw her last and when. That could help eliminate some people from his list if they had an alibi for the time of her disappearance. But he had to narrow that timeline down.

The non-profit was located on Grant Avenue and Bryan headed there, his mind formulating a plan to get maximum effect with as little effort as he could. Get her colleagues all together and weed them out one by one.

As he was turning into the parking area, his phone rang. The number said unknown.

He clicked accept and waited. “Mr. Gamble?” a male voice said.

“Yes. Who is this?”

“Sanderson Emery. My assistant said you stopped by and wanted to talk to me about Charlene? What is this concerning?”

Bryan sighed with relief. “Thank you for calling. I wanted to know when you last spoke with her.”

“Why? Is something wrong?” Was there concern in his tone? It was hard to gauge.

“We’re not sure yet. No one seems to be able to get hold of her. When did you speak to her last?”

“Saturday night, around nine. She was out with a friend, having a few drinks.”

“Can you tell me who this friend was?”

“Felicity Jordan, I believe. The two work together at her non-profit.”

“And you haven’t tried to reach her since?”

“I just got back into town today. I was in Madrid for work. She and I had an agreement that if either of us were out of the country, we’d wait to talk after we returned.

Most of my overseas trips give me little time to breathe, let alone spend time on the phone."

To Bryan, their relationship sounded more friendly than romantic but then again, what did he know? He hadn't been in one for years.

"So, nothing since Saturday night?"

"We talked as I was boarding my plane. Pretty much a hello and goodbye." Bryan detected no real alarm in the man's voice. Why?

"Thank you again for calling me back. I do appreciate it."

"You will let me know when you hear from her, won't you?"

Bryan cleared his throat. "Yes, as long as you do the same."

"Will do," he said, then the phone went dead.

Bryan parked and exited his truck, his mind whirling a mile a minute. Inside, he needed to find Felicity first and speak to her about their night out. She may just be able to give him the timeframe he needed to compare alibis.

He stepped up to the desk where a petite brunette in a short, red dress sat, filing her nails. When she looked up, her hazel eyes seemed to do a double-take.

"Hello." He gave the woman his best dimply smile. "I need to speak to Felicity Jordan if she's available."

"May I tell her who is asking?"

"Sure. Bryan Gamble and I'm here to talk to her about Charlene Reed."

"Charlie? What about her? She hasn't been to work in two days. Do you know why?"

"I'm not at liberty to say. Is Felicity here?"

"Let me call her." She picked up the phone and

pressed nine. "Someone at the front desk is here to see you." She placed the phone back on the base. "She's on her way. You can take a seat if you'd like."

"No, thank you." Bryan had sat long enough that day. He wasn't going to do it again. Instead, he turned and glanced at the pictures on the wall, one drawing him in. It was Charlie. A much clearer picture than the one he got in the packet he received.

As he stared at her, he swallowed past the lump forming in his throat. The woman looked nothing like her father. She had a head of fiery red hair, masses of long curls framing a face that had him mesmerized. The irises of her eyes were a strange yet fascinating shade of violet. Bryan had never met anyone with such stunning eyes before, and it caused a ripple in his pulse rate.

Charlie's nose was pert and slightly upturned, her rose-colored lips full and pouty. The woman literally took his breath away, a reaction Bryan had never experienced before. Especially from a photograph.

"She's beautiful, isn't she?" a female voice said from behind him, drawing him away from Charlie's picture.

"Yes, she is," he said, studying the woman in front of him, stunning in her own right. African American, with black hair, shining like onyx. Her eyes were a light shade of amber, a kindness reflecting through that had Bryan immediately at ease.

"You must be Felicity?"

"I am. And you are?"

"Bryan Gamble and I'm here to talk to you about Saturday night. You were out with Charlie. Can you tell me when you two parted ways?"

Her eyes widened. "What happened to her? When

she didn't return my text on Monday morning, I knew something was wrong. I just didn't know what to do."

"We don't know much. That's why I need to know exactly what time you saw her last."

"It was around eleve -thirty Saturday night outside the Oasis Bar and Grill. I wanted to walk her to her car, but she said she'd be fine. That it was just up the street. Who do you work for?"

"We are working for her father," he said, not sure he should mention Bolton's Valor at this point. "He's worried about her since she hasn't returned any of his calls, and that isn't like her."

"Exactly. She always returns my texts, and I know she and her father are very close. If she was able to call him, she would."

Bryan watched for body language. "Do you know if Charlie was mentoring anyone whose husband might be angry with her. Perhaps would want to harm her?"

"Oh my God. Yes. Leon Sherman has threatened her. Said she needed to get his wife Evelyne to come back to him."

"Do you have an address for this man?"

"I do. Let me go get it. First, is there anything I can do here?"

"Talk to all your coworkers. See if any of them have heard from Charlie."

"Already did. No one has talked to her since Friday afternoon."

"One follow-up question. Did Charlie get a call from her boyfriend while the two of you were out?" Bryan wanted confirmation on what Emery told him.

Her eyes narrowed. "What boyfriend?"

"Sanderson Emery. I spoke to him right before I

entered the building. He told me he talked to Charlie around nine that night. He was boarding a flight for Madrid at the time."

"Yes, she did speak to Sanderson on the phone around that time, but the two are only friends. No benefits are involved." For whatever reason, this knowledge caused a flutter in Bryan's gut.

"Then why does her father think they are romantic?"

"Well, that's a story I'm not sure Charlie would want me to reveal."

"If I'm to find her, I need to know as much as possible. Anything you tell me won't go past us. You have my word."

"Okay. Charlie and Sanderson met at a charity function five months ago and got to talking about how hard it was to live a normal life, with him being so rich, and her daddy being on some of the most influential committees in Congress. You draw in all kinds of people, some good, some looking for a way in. They made a pact that night to pretend to be dating to take the pressure off both of them."

"But she didn't tell her father? Why?"

"Because she knew he'd tell her to not worry about his position. To just live her life. She wanted to protect him, and using Sanderson as her pretend boyfriend could help with that."

"Does anyone else know about this?"

"Just me on Charlie's end. I don't know about Sanderson's."

"All right, so if they aren't dating, could there be someone else in her life—someone she could be with right now?"

"No. She would have told me. I'm her best friend.

Something bad happened. I feel it in my bones."

"Then we're back to this client's husband. Run and get that man's address, and I'll go check him out."

****

Charlie shook her head, trying to stave off this strange grogginess she woke up with. Not thinking, she'd eaten some of the food her abductor had brought and then became drowsy and fell asleep. She had no idea how much time had passed, but she was pretty sure the food had been drugged. Probably to keep her from causing trouble. From now on, she wouldn't touch whatever he served. She had to keep a clear head so she could find a way to escape.

Footsteps nearing had her on alert. Her kidnapper was coming. Good luck having her fall for being drugged again. He was going to have to come up with another way for her to stay compliant.

The door rattled and light filtered in. The man was again wearing the ghoulish mask, dressed all in black, making any identification impossible if she did manage to get free. Not a dumb guy for sure. Clearly not a kidnapping of convenience but a well-planned one. That worried her even more.

He stepped in and placed another tray in front of her. This time, along with the food, there was a package of wipes and two plastic water bottles. She was parched, but was the water drugged as well? How could she know for sure?

"We have yet to get a hold of your father. Seems he's out of the office. You better hope within the next twelve hours, he gets back to us, or you are going to become a liability real fast."

An idea struck Charlie. "Why not text him from my

phone? You surely have it since it was in my handbag."

The man chuckled. "You mean so they can track where you are? That sim card came out and was tossed the second we had you. Don't think we can be outsmarted, Ms. Reed. You'll be disappointed."

Charlie stared daggers at the man, suddenly more angry than scared. This asshole was going to pay when he was caught. She was going to make sure of that. But first, she had to get out of there in one piece, and to do that, she needed to bide her time, act complacent, then spring.

He left, and she sat back contemplating if the water was safe to drink or not. Surely, if the seal wasn't broken, then it was probably not tampered with. Her mouth was as dry as the Sahara, and dehydration would make her weak and not be able to think straight, something she needed right now for her to get out and run for help.

Charlie was going to take a chance and drink the water. She picked up one bottle and examined the seal, the plastic tabs looking broken.

Shit. He seriously wanted her to sleep through this whole abduction. She grabbed the other bottle and didn't see any broken tabs and prayed that it was safe. Charlie removed the cap and drank the water, not noticing any bitter taste. A drug in food would be easier to hide. Water would be much harder.

Now, she had to come up with a plan to get out of there without getting killed. But how? *Think. Think. Think, Charlie. You can do this. Daddy taught you skills. Use them.*

Charlie was lucky; her father was ex-military, and after her mother died in a car wreck when she was fifteen, he'd taught her to defend herself in every situation. Unless she was knocked out cold like they'd done. Maybe if she'd been sober, she could have reacted, but with two drinks in her, she'd failed. Her father would be so upset with her for letting her guard down. Now, she was a prisoner to these men, which she knew was more than one from the voices she'd heard, all because she refused to let Felicity accompany her to her car at the end of the block. Stupid when women were targeted if they were alone. Perhaps she wouldn't be in this mess if she had.

Chapter 3

Bryan sat in his truck outside Leon Sherman's apartment complex, unsure if he was even there. He had no idea what the man drove, only that he lived in apartment sixteen.

He blew out a ragged breath and exited his SUV, trying to figure out what to say if indeed the man was home. Should he lie and say he was there to talk to him about his wife, Evelyne, or should he be straightforward and ask about his whereabouts on Saturday night when Charlie disappeared?

Bryan was just going to wing it and hope he could tell if the man was lying to him or not.

At the door, he knocked and waited. After a moment, he knocked again, then glanced at his phone. Maybe this guy wasn't off work yet.

He'd call Sterling and ask him to do a background check, find out where he worked, what kind of car he drove. Anything that would be pertinent to finding the man's location.

Until then, he'd go check out Charlie's apartment and see if there were any clues there. Perhaps she had made it to her place that night, and something happened then. This way, he could cross that off his list.

On his way there, he called Sterling. He should have utilized his skills sooner to learn what he could on Sherman. It wouldn't happen again.

"What do you need, Bryan?" Sterling asked as soon as he picked up. "Can you find everything you can on Leon Sherman? His wife is Evelyne."

"I'm on it."

"Thanks."

"No need to thank me. This is my job. Give me an hour and I'll get back to you. Do you want me to ping his phone too?"

"If you can, yes. I need to locate him."

"Okay."

Bryan programmed Charlie's address into his navigational system and pulled out of the complex. She lived in Monterey Bay, a gated condo community for the upper-middle class. Bryan had only driven by the place, too expensive for any ex-military man. A senator's daughter, not so much. Hell, Daddy probably even paid for it since there wasn't much money in working for a non-profit.

"Take the next left onto Bedrock," his navigation said, drawing his attention to make the turn. He and Charlie couldn't come from anymore different backgrounds. His father was a drunk, his mother too tired from working twelve-hour shifts to care about him having a worthwhile childhood. He didn't blame her for that—he blamed his no-good father, who thought drinking was more important than holding onto a job. Catherine Gamble had supported all three of them on her nurse's salary and had died way too young because of it. The man, who he didn't claim as a father and hadn't seen in ten years, was still alive and kicking. Go figure.

Bryan shook off the negative thoughts as he neared the gate to Monterey Bay. There was a keycard in the packet, and he grabbed for it, sliding it into the reader, and the gate opened to allow him in.

She lived in condo eight. He pulled up into her driveway and cut the engine. No car was there. That meant she didn't make it back here. Was it still parked a block from the Oasis? He'd need to check to be sure. Bryan was still going to go inside in case something was there to lead him to her abductor.

Off the seat, he retrieved the spare key her father had and walked to the door. She had a security system that he'd have to punch a set of numbers into once inside.

On the other side of the door, he went straight for the unit and pressed in the six digits.

He blew out a breath and looked around, stunned by how immaculate the place appeared. Did the woman have a housekeeper, or did she keep it this way herself? His place was clean, but not like this. It didn't even look lived in. Maybe she was never home.

He went from room to room, all as sparkling as the front. Not a speck of dust anywhere. Maybe not having a real social life gave her ample time to clean like this. Did the woman ever relax? It sure as hell didn't look like it.

In her bedroom, he walked to her closet and opened the door, finding a walk-in unit where everything was coordinated by color, her shoes in high-end, clear boxes. On the end stood a mahogany stand that just fit below the top shelf of the closet, where there were at least twenty handbags in an array of vibrant hues—all designer, he was sure.

He walked over and glanced inside a few of the ten-drawer boxes, and was shocked at how many pieces of jewelry she possessed. All this stuff suggested the woman loved to shop.

Bryan had always been a minimalist since he'd spent fifteen years in the military, enlisting right out of high school. Another obvious difference between them. Charlie might be the prettiest woman Bryan had ever seen, but they had zero in common.

He left the closet, walked to her nightstand and opened the top drawer. There was a stack of letters held together by a thick rubber band. Who could they be from? Would it be an invasion of privacy to look? Whoever wrote them probably had nothing to do with her disappearance. Maybe he'd simply glance at the sender—and keep it in mind if he got nowhere with Sherman.

He picked up the pile and glanced at the name, instantly taken aback. Nathan Beal. Wasn't he some kind of hotshot political advisor? Bryan was going to need to find out if he worked on her father's campaign. Was Charlie having an affair with the man? Could she be with him right now?

He dug out his phone and called Sterling again. "Sorry, don't have everything on him yet."

"I need you to also find out everything you can on Nathan Beal. He might have been secretly seeing Charlie."

"Which one do you want first?"

"Get me the location on Leon Sherman now. Then you can find out everything you can on Beal."

"I'm on it. I'll call you right back."

Bryan tucked his phone into his pocket and continued the search of her condo.

At least now he had another avenue to follow. Was Charlie having a sordid fling with Beal behind her father's back? The man had to be twenty years older than her—what would she have seen in him? The whole thing was bizarre. But then again, Bryan was hardly an expert on women and their behaviors. He only dated a handful of them, and never seriously. Work had always been his focus since a family was not something he wanted after his upbringing. After all, with his unstable childhood, who in their right mind would?

****

Charlie crept to the door, turned the handle and found it locked. *Dammit.* How was she going to get out of there? Could she overpower her abductor next time he came through the door? She had some skills in jujitsu, but what if he had more? The guy was twice her size. That alone left her at a huge disadvantage.

She needed to use her brain. That was her best asset. Charlie knew she could outsmart him even though he'd implied otherwise. She just needed the confidence to try. But she had to see an opportunity first. The man couldn't see it coming. To do that, she needed to appear too frightened to look like a threat, and then be able to get past the other guy there. Seemed like an impossible feat, but somehow, she had to find a way before she became the liability the captor spoke of.

She went back to sit down, grabbing for the package of wipes. Maybe being somewhat cleaner would make her feel better. Her hair was a matted mess, to the point that she couldn't even get her fingers through the curls. It was going to take days to fix once she was back home. Just another reason to be irate, if she could even be angrier than she already was at this point.

Perhaps she needed to think about who would use her against her father. He was chairman on two committees: the Judiciary Committee and

Appropriations. What would someone have to gain if he voted a certain way? This was exactly the reason she chose to pretend to be dating Sanderson, to try and avoid any influence over her father. Now, here she was at the hands of men who wanted to do just that—have her father compromised.

Somehow, she had to get out of there before that could happen. Her father could lose his job if anyone found out, and his career meant everything to him. She was the only person he'd risk it for, and no way could she let that happen. Charlie loved him more than herself. She would die before she'd allow him to lose everything he had worked so hard for.

She opened the package, pulled out a wipe and ran it up and down her arms, the scent, a floral tone. Charlie guessed the guy coming in was starting to find her offensive.

Fuck him.

If she didn't care, she'd stay this way, but she was a clean freak, always had been. Not being able to take a shower was killing her.

Charlie continued to clean as much as she could of herself, using at least ten wipes, then sat back and mulled over some of the committees her dad was on. What was coming up in each that his vote a certain way would matter? Or a person being called to testify before him? Could it be that simple? Charlie had no idea.

She slid over and leaned against the far wall, her back and butt starting to hurt. How much longer were they going to keep her here in this dark, uncomfortable place?

Charlie wanted to be home, in her bed, a need so strong she pictured herself there, her cashmere blanket tucked around her, the scent of lavender emitting from the diffuser on her nightstand. That scent always relaxed her and helped her sleep. She could almost smell it in the air, so much so that her eyes slid closed.

A noise startled her awake. She focused forward, her gaze landing on the man in the mask standing in the doorway, staring at her. Her skin goose bumped as he remained quiet, just watching her.

"What do you want?" she asked in a sharp tone.

"Just wanted you to know your father has finally responded to our calls. Not sure he'll do what we want of him yet. How much does he love you?"

She shook her head, trying to figure out what was going on. "What did you ask him to do?"

"You don't need to know that. But if he doesn't, we may have to give him a little incentive. Maybe one of your fingers, perhaps."

Charlie gasped, the mere idea causing her body to go cold. This creep was going to cut off a finger if her father didn't comply. How long was her dad going to be given before that happened? This just upped her need to escape. Next time he came in, she was going to spring. She had to be ready to attack because she wasn't going to let him dismember any of her digits, not if she could help it.

Chapter 4

"I'm looking for Charlene Reed. I have reason to believe you might know where she is?" Bryan asked, staring hard at the man, who he'd finally located outside Hanover's, where he worked as a carpenter.

Leon Sherman's face reddened, and his fists clenched at his side. "Why would I know where that bitch is? I haven't seen her since the day after she hid my wife from me."

"Some of her coworkers heard you threaten her life, and now she's missing. This doesn't look good for you, Leon. Maybe you should just come clean now. Where is she?"

"I have no fucking idea. Like I said, last time I saw her, she'd helped my wife take my two kids away. Haven't seen her since. If you do find her, tell her I hope she chokes on her own bile."

Bryan wanted to punch the shit out of this abuser but thought better of it. Last thing he needed was an assault on his record. Vince would not be happy with that.

One thing though, he believed Sherman was telling the truth. He had no idea where Charlie was. Yet another person to cross off his list of suspects. Now, Nathan Beal was on deck. Hopefully, Sterling had found some info on the man and where he could find him.

He walked away from Sherman, pressed call on his contact page and waited.

"Just got all the info you'll need on Beal," Sterling said immediately. "He did work on Senator Reed's campaign. He is still a consultant for him. He lives in Denver. But activity on his platinum card suggests he's here in Winding Creek, staying at the Pembroke Inn."

Bryan knew the place—the most expensive inn in the area. Only the very wealthy could step through those doors. Hopefully, he could get to Beal somewhere else, since security there was impossible to get past. He'd learned that the first week on the job, while tailing a suspect there. Perhaps he'd wait for him to step out the door. First, though, he was going to drive to the Oasis and see if Charlie's car was a block away and look for any available security cameras. Maybe, he'd get lucky and catch her abduction on tape. See who grabbed her and hope he could identify them somehow.

"Were you able to ping his phone?" Bryan asked as an afterthought.

"No. He must have it turned off."

Why would he do that? Unless he was busy having a liaison with a woman and didn't want any distractions.

"Okay. Thanks, Sterling."

"No problem. If I get a ping, I'll call you."

"All right." Bryan clicked end and googled the Oasis's address, then punched it into his navigation and took off. This was probably a dead-end, but he had to try everything he could think of to find her. She was probably running out of time. He had to locate her before something horrific happened.

It took Bryan ten minutes to get to the Oasis and another two to find Charlie's car. The doors were locked, which suggested she didn't make it there. They got her somewhere in between. Now, he'd look around for any kind of surveillance cameras. It was a long shot, sure, but he was going to do it anyway.

He glanced left to right, noting an area that would be the perfect place to grab someone. The surroundings would be completely dark from either side. This was probably where they snatched her.

Bryan glanced down at the ground and noticed where it looked like drag marks on the asphalt and a type of hairpin.

He reached to pick it up and rolled it over in his hand. He'd bet money it was Charlie's. Also, he saw a footprint, which looked to be about a size twelve and a half, close to where the pin was located. That meant the guy was probably big in size. That would exclude Leon Sherman and Sanderson Emery, who were inches from being six feet. He wasn't sure about Beal. He'd need height and weight on him from Sterling.

Again, Bryan looked up and saw a camera that might have caught something on it, though it was dark in the spot where she was taken. Maybe he'd get lucky and see something he could use. The camera was for a pawn shop's back entrance. He walked to the door and entered, thinking that he'd even pay the man to get access to the footage if he had to.

He stepped up to the counter and waited. The owner must be in the back office.

Bryan dinged the bell on the glass counter and stood back and looked around. Inside another glass case, were a bunch of rings, one that caught his eye. It not only had a cluster of diamonds but rubies as well, in a silver setting. It was perfect to give a woman as a wedding ring.

"Can I help you?" a man asked, startling Bryan.

The man was thin, in his mid-thirties with a long

beard. "Yes. Thanks. I noticed you have a security camera pointing toward the alley out back. A woman was abducted three nights ago. Would it be possible for me to see the footage from that night?"

The man gave him a sheepish grin. "Well, that all depends."

"On?"

"If you plan on buying that ring you were eying."

Bryan was shocked by the suggestion. Quite the businessman he was dealing with here. "Okay. How much for the ring?"

"It's an heirloom."

"Right."

"With diamonds and rubies."

"I saw that."

"In an amazing setting."

Byran didn't have time to haggle. "Just tell me how much you want."

"Four hundred dollars."

Damn. That was a lot of money for him. But he'd pay it if that meant seeing the footage. "Sold."

He handed the man his credit card.

The owner rang him up and placed the ring in a box and bag.

"Now can I see the camera footage from three nights ago?"

"Absolutely. Follow me."

Bryan was led into a room in the back and given access to the footage. "Take your time."

He found that night's footage and sped through until Charlie and Felicity parted ways. The picture was dark, but he could still see the alleyway clearly. Movement caused him to move closer, where he saw Charlie heading down the alley, digging in her purse, probably for her keys. Two men sprang out from behind a dumpster, one tall and slim, the other shorter, heavyset, with a limp.

Bryan zoomed in closer to get a clear picture on his phone of both men. Now, he had to find out who they were. Maybe facial recognition software would help. He'd text Sterling the pictures and hoped the man could identify them somehow. If not, he was back to square one.

****

Charlie was done with this whole situation. It was time to get the hell out of there. The masked man had come back with yet another tray hours ago, the food was probably drugged again. She hadn't touched it. She had to be alert since she was finding a way out of this room one way or the other. Alive or dead—whatever applied. Now, she had to wait for him to return, no matter how long she had to stand next to the door.

She wished she knew what was beyond this room. What was outside? A city street or somewhere in the country. She had no idea, but come hell or high water, she was going to find out.

It couldn't be any worse than where she was now. Trapped with lunatics who wanted to sever one of her fingers if her father didn't comply with their demands.

What had they asked him to do?

Ransom was one thing, but using his powers of congress was altogether another. That would compromise him and his career. Charlie couldn't allow it. Not when she knew how important he was to the country. They needed him right where he was, not having to resign because of her.

Footsteps echoed down the hall, and she held her breath, praying she could overpower this guy and get past the other. No easy feat for sure, but she needed to try. Otherwise, she was just waiting to die.

The steps neared, and she held her breath as she watched the doorknob turn. When he started to enter, she slammed both her fists into his stomach, then kicked him hard in the groin, causing him to double over and collapse on the ground.

Charlie didn't hesitate. She closed the door and sent the bolt lock in place. Now she had to escape the other abductor and get out and hope she could find help quickly, before they came after her.

She moved slowly down a short hallway, noting sunlight filtering in from somewhere. She hadn't seen anything but darkness for at least two days, maybe three if she'd slept through one.

At the end of the hallway, she peeked around, not seeing anyone. Ahead of her was a door she was sure would lead her outside.

She took a breath and sprinted for the exit, opening it to find trees and brush everywhere. Charlie had hoped she was still in the city. But that wasn't the case and hardly mattered now. She couldn't stand there. She had to run.

She raced for the tree line, zigzagging, trying to get as much distance from what looked like some type of cabin as she could. Was it owned by her abductor or someone else's that they'd broken into?

Voices from behind indicated that they were trying to get to her. She had to hide until they passed. But where? She glanced around, spotting a downed tree. She shot to the aspen, tucking herself close to the side, burying herself with fallen leaves. The roughness of the bark dug into her skin, but this would be nothing compared to what would happen if they caught her again. She needed to stay hidden and hope they gave up and left.

Rustling of leaves had her holding her breath, praying they wouldn't find her.

"Do you see her?" the other man, who she hadn't seen, asked.

"No. Where the fuck did she go? He's going to be so angry if we let her escape."

Who was the *he* they were talking about?

Here she thought these two were behind the abduction. Now she knew it was someone else.

Chapter 5

Bryan studied the profile of both men who had kidnapped Charlie, trying to figure out why either would have any reason to take her. From what he could surmise, they were two idiots who worked at a warehouse loading and unloading freight. The whole thing made no sense. Perhaps through, they were hired to abduct her. That could very well be. But by who and why? That was the question that needed to be answered after he found her and brought her to safety.

As Bryan waited, Sterling was getting info on the cars they drove and finding out if their GPS systems or phones could locate either of them. If nothing else, it could get Bryan closer to Charlie.

His phone rang and he picked up. “We got a location on both men. They are together in the Rocky Mountain National Park. I’ll send you the coordinates.”

Bryan blew out a relieved breath. Now, he could get to her. His phone dinged a text, and Bryan put the info into his navigation and then took off. It’d take him an hour to get to where he’d have to go on foot the rest of the way. Thankfully, he always carried a go bag in the back of his SUV. It was a survivalist’s wet dream of everything needed to get by for a week anywhere in the world.

He took the merge onto the highway headed for Estes Park, the nearest town to where he’d get access to the forest entrance.

Five minutes led to ten, then an hour as he got off the highway and entered his hometown, picturesque to say the least. This was Bryan's first time back since his return from service. His father still lived here, a man who he would always blame for his mother's death. Funny that it took the man four months after her demise to latch onto yet another gullible woman to marry and to take care of him. Disgusting to say the least. Bryan refused to ever be that pathetic.

Shaking the thought, he drove to the entrance of the forest and parked. Inside the area was a truck with a trailer—no doubt Charlie's abductors. This was where he traveled up the mountain on foot.

He punched the GPS coordinates into his phone and got out, grabbed his go bag and the Glock from its case, then locked his car. It'd take him about two hours of uphill terrain to get to where their cell phone pings came from. But it was all worth it as long as he found Charlie alive.

Bryan started up the incline, too hyped to take in the scenery. All he could think about was what would happen once he reached his destination. Were her abductors armed? That was his only concern since he knew he could take them out if they weren't packing. His fighting skills were top-notch, and one of the men had an obvious disability. Easily beatable in hand-to-hand combat.

His foot slipped, and he caught himself before going down. It was getting steeper, which meant he needed to focus on every step he took.

The two who had Charlie clearly had to have a four-wheeler, much easier to get to wherever they held her. If he'd had more time, he might have considered one himself, but she'd been their captive too long already, and he had to find her.

Minute by minute, Bryan trudged up the mountain, each step careful and precise. His weapon was tucked in the waist of his pants. When he got closer to the coordinates, he'd take it out.

After an hour and a half of traveling, faint voices had him stopping in his tracks. They were echoing from up the mountain. What the hell were they shouting about?

He started moving again, listening intently, hoping to find out what was going on. If they'd abducted Charlie, you'd think they'd want to lie low, not try and draw attention to themselves. Then again, they were this far up. Perhaps they weren't worried about being discovered.

Bryan crept forward. He needed to stay as quiet as he could while moving toward the voices. He didn't want to alert them to his location. As the voices drew closer, he could make out what they were saying. Charlie had escaped. This was going to make things harder for him. He couldn't simply start shooting when she could be anywhere, possibly get hit. His best bet was to somehow find her first, and that was going to be like locating a needle in a haystack. This mountain was vast, and she could be anywhere.

As he moved in, he spotted one of the men, the one with the limp searching around him. Strapped to the man's back was an AR-15. So, they were packing heat. Could he take him out without a shot being fired or the other man showing up to aid him? Probably not. That meant that he needed to find Charlie and try to get them out of there without the two even knowing he was here.

This was his wheelhouse, trying to evade the enemy. He dropped to the ground and crawled to the nearest tree, looking left to right, wondering how Charlie had managed to get away from these two men. He'd need to give her mad props. But then, knowing her father's background, Dennis probably taught her everything he knew and that would help once he found her.

****

Charlie knew she couldn't stay where she was forever, especially when she had no idea what time of day it was. Staying until it was dark could be hours away, and once it was, which direction would she go? She could find herself traveling farther away from help, and where would that get her?

She knew she would have to start moving, but she'd wait until the voices were at a distance. Right now, she had to keep her wits about her, think like her father would. All the combat action he'd seen during Desert Storm and the invasion of Afghanistan and Iraq had helped him teach her how to stay alive and she needed to use that knowledge now. Though, the terrain and temps involved here were different. At night, the mountains could get frigid this time of year. Hopefully, she wouldn't freeze to death trying to evade being captured again.

The men's voices were farther away, and she uncovered herself and crawled to the nearest tree and glanced up, trying to get her bearings. She didn't have a compass, but the sun rose in the east and would move west. So, she would go the opposite way to get down the mountain. Charlie glanced up again and then took a calming breath and crawled down to the next tree and then another, each move getting her farther from the voices.

When they were at a clear distance, she stood and started to run.

While passing a tree, someone grabbed her around her waist and mouth and dragged her into a rocky area that was an inlet of sorts and was blocked from view. She struggled to get free, flailing her arms and legs, her foot connecting with his shin, causing him to grunt.

His grip loosened and she took that opportunity to break free and sprint forward, only to have him catch her again, this time saying, “Your father sent me.”

She instantly stopped and looked at him.

He put his finger to his lips to indicate not to say anything. She nodded and followed him back to the rocky structure. It was a place to stay hidden since the male voices were now getting closer again.

Charlie held her breath, feeling safe for the first time in days. This man was there to save her at her father’s behest, and that’s all she needed to know.

“We are going to have to call him and tell him she escaped,” the man who came to deliver her food said. “He’s probably going to refuse to pay us now.”

“You should have kept the bitch tied up the whole time.”

“He didn’t want that. That was the reason we drugged her food. She was supposed to sleep until her father complied. He didn’t want her to suffer in any way.”

Who was this guy? He clearly cared if she was hurt but still kidnapped her to get something from her father. What could that be? She had to figure it out.

The voices were moving away again, and she released a breath, relaxing her tense body against the man sent to rescue her.

For moments, he stayed still, probably trying to get his bearings. Once they started moving, both would need to be as quiet as they could while working their way down the mountain.

He squeezed her shoulder and pointed to another tree about one hundred yards away. He then grasped her hand and started to move in its direction, not at a run but a fast walk. Charlie was thankful that she was active and could keep up, though her isolation and lack of food made her weak.

They reached the tree, the trunk large enough to hide them both from sight. Now what? His moves were clearly thought out, suggesting he, too, was ex-military. He rubbed her arm and pointed toward a rock formation.

Charlie nodded, and the two shot out toward the structure, relieved when they were tucked behind it. This was going to be a slow process, but the man knew how to stay out of sight.

She watched him look around and tip his head toward another large tree, this time two hundred yards ahead. They sprinted this time, the base coming none too soon. Charlie was winded, which would hinder them if it kept up. It had to be the drugs and lack of food and water in her system. But she had to fight it, or her captors would catch them and that was the last thing in the world she wanted to happen.

Chapter 6

Bryan could tell Charlie was struggling to keep up with him. Did her kidnappers deprive her of food and water? Was this why she was so weak? Thankfully, it would be dark soon. He'd need to find a place to lie low for the night. Then he could get her to eat and drink something and rest until first light.

Off in the distance, he saw another deep rock formation. He pointed it out to her, and she nodded. They dashed forward, zigzagging here and there to avoid larger fir saplings and slick areas that could bring them down.

When they reached the boulders, Bryan was happy to see that there was a set of rocks that would keep them hidden even from the front. This was where they would settle in for the night. He hadn't heard any voices for at least fifteen minutes. He wasn't sure if that was a good or bad thing. He'd have to wait and see.

Once they were tucked behind the rocks, he took off his backpack, unzipped a pouch and handed her a bottle of power water. It would get some electrolytes in her and help her body recover.

She gave him a weak smile and twisted the cap off, and drank a large gulp.

He worked his way into another pocket and found two MREs, choosing the one that he thought best for her. A hearty beef stew and a chocolate brownie for dessert.

He picked another for himself, not remembering the last time he ate. He'd been too busy trying to find Charlie. Thank God he had. Now, he just needed to get them off this mountain and somewhere safe until they learned who orchestrated this kidnapping. Because he knew it wasn't the two men who had her. Her abductors said as much.

Once they were headed back to Winding Creek, he'd start asking questions. Hopefully, he and Charlie could figure out who would have something to gain by using a US congressman. Was it to vote a certain way, or to cancel a congressional subpoena for an upcoming hearing? Bryan didn't know, but he sure as hell was going to find out once they were back at Bolton's offices. They had a huge panic room there where Charlie could stay until all this was cleared up and people were arrested.

She took the foil pouch he handed her, opened it and ate like she hadn't in days. So much for not doing harm. The two clearly hadn't followed orders. Otherwise, she wouldn't be starving.

As Byran ate his food, he studied her. Her auburn hair was an unruly mess, but it still didn't detract from her beauty. After days of being at the mercy of these animals, she looked clean, actually smelled like flowers.

He wished it was safe to talk to her—hear her voice for the first time. But that was going to have to wait until they were in his vehicle and getting as far away from these hired idiots as possible.

He took a bite of his food, not at all turned off by the taste. He was used to pre-packaged meals since serving over fifteen years in the army. His palate was used to them. Some were good, especially when traveling miles and miles with a hundred-pound pack on your back.

Once both had finished their food, he cleared away the mess, sticking it in a bag, and then reached in to grab the thermal blanket neatly folded inside another zippered compartment. The two would have to share, but it would keep them warm.

Bryan and a few friends had done the overnight in these mountains. This time of year, it could dip low. They would need to stay close. The mere idea caused his body to respond. *Dammit.* What the hell was wrong with him? She had just been kidnapped. She didn't need yet another man trying to touch her in any way other than to keep her safe.

He tucked the blanket over her and waited for her to get comfortable, then leaned against a rock to stand watch, at least for another few hours. The hired kidnappers would have to wait for morning since finding them in the dark would be virtually impossible. Hopefully, once it was light out, he'd have Charlie halfway down the mountain and as far away from this nightmare as possible.

****

A buzzing noise startled Charlie awake. A strong, masculine body lay next to her, almost lulling her back to sleep. His scent had a hint of sandalwood and pine—intoxicating to her senses.

Warm breath touched her ear. "Don't move," he said, his voice deep and stirring something strange inside her belly.

What was going on? What was that strange humming sound?

He covered both their heads with the blanket as the buzzing got closer, sounding like it was above them. Was it a drone? And was it up there to search for them?

Fuck. This was not good. This gave them an advantage—an extra set of eyes to find them. How were they going to stay hidden with this thing flying around them?

When she'd first opened her eyes, she'd seen a glimpse of light, the sun rising in the east. They could have started moving again, now they were stuck under this blanket. But for how long? Were they going to be able to get away, or would they be captured?

He whispered again. "When it moves away, we are going to start running. If it gets close again, we'll drop down and cover ourselves, okay?"

"Okay," she said, taking a long breath.

Under the blanket, she could see him tuck his arms through his backpack.

The hum started to move away.

They rose and sprinted to a set of trees, hiding behind them, both looking up to see where the drone had gone.

He pointed to it off in the distance, then took her hand and pulled her in the opposite direction, racing into a deep set of firs. He was smart and was keeping them in the denseness. That way, they couldn't be spotted from above. If they could stay under the cover of trees, the two might be able to get down the mountain and away from these guys. That was a big if.

He tapped her on the shoulder and directed her toward another grouping of trees, and they shot out and raced toward them, gasping for air once they'd reached the clustering. Her rescuer was in great physical shape. She was struggling to say the least. Yes, she worked out on a regular basis, but wasn't used to this kind of excursion, especially in this elevation. The air was thinner, and it was harder for her to breathe.

He tilted his head toward the trees ahead, and they raced for the grouping, the humming getting closer again.

He squatted down and tugged her with him. She held her breath as the drone hovered above them. Had they been spotted? She didn't know, but this holding pattern was causing every nerve in her body to charge. What type of cameras were on this device? Was it military grade or a simple, box store, toy type? Hopefully the latter. They didn't have the range the ones used by the military did. Charlie only knew this because of her father.

Finally, the thing started to move, and she released her breath. The man beside her tugged her arm and pointed down a steep embankment to a large rock formation. They shot out, ascending the mountain, Charlie almost slipping on rocks that started to slide. He caught her before going down and they kept going, reaching the rocks without another incident.

He covered them with the silver blanket that camouflaged them from view. "I hear it coming again. It's using a grid search pattern from what I've seen so far. That suggests it's military grade. We'll stay here until it leaves."

Dammit. Who would have access to this type of hardware? That knew her father? If she could figure that out, she'd know who kidnapped her and what they had to gain by it.

Chapter 7

Bryan knew whoever abducted Charlie was someone with a wide reach. Not just anyone could get their hands on a military drone. That alone had his head spinning.

Once they were down the mountain, he was going to spend the drive to Bolton's grilling Charlie on who had something to gain by controlling a congressman—someone who knew Dennis and Charlie's life.

Sanderson had tons of money. He could get access to a high-grade drone like this, but what would he need from the congressman? That was the million-dollar question for the billionaire himself. Who else could have abducted her, known where she was to tell these idiots to wait for her in that alleyway outside the Oasis? Bryan was going to have to look at him closer. Did he travel to Madrid just to have an alibi for the abduction? Bryan needed to find out.

The drone started to move away. It was time to get going, or they'd never get to his vehicle. "Let's go," he said, jumping up and helping her rise.

Bryan scanned the area, spotting another large cluster of trees, pointing to them. They raced toward the firs, his ears perking up when he heard voices off in the distance. Clearly, the drone technician must have spotted them and told them where they were.

Now, he was going to have to keep them moving

until they could lay low.

"Run," he whispered to her, her eyes wide with fear. She heard the voices, too, and knew they were in trouble.

Bryan led them out from under cover, down a steep embankment and across a clearing to another set of trees as the drone came closer again. He squatted down, and she did the same, trying to make them unnoticeable. While they waited for the drone to pass, Bryan searched for a place to hide. The abductors were getting closer. Even though they were no longer talking, he could hear them stomping through the woods—heard rocks sliding.

He'd learned how to be quiet in any situation on his first tour in Afghanistan. Bryan could be stealthy, but he had Charlie, and that was going to make this more difficult. Best to find a hiding place now and stay until he knew they were no longer in ear and eye shot of them. This two-hour trip down the mountain was going to take days with them and that drone above. Thank God he had enough supplies to last a while because it might take a long time to get to safety without getting shot. AR-15s could spray bullets up to six-hundred yards. The chances of getting hit were too high. No way could he take that chance. Charlie was precious cargo, and he was going to protect her with his life.

Down the hill was an area he wanted to explore. It could be where they could stay for a while. He pointed it out to her, and she nodded. The two rushed out of the trees and sprinted to the brushy area and he dragged her under the leafy canvas, crawling deep into the middle, completely hidden from everything. She was forced to stay right next to him, her arm bumped up against his. The mere contact caused blood to rush through his veins. There was something about this woman that had his body going haywire—a reaction he'd never experienced before. Was it just an adrenaline thing from their circumstances or was it something more? Bryan wasn't sure, but he knew he didn't appreciate it right now when he was trying to keep a cool head. He had to get her out of here alive, and this reaction to her wasn't helping.

The crunching close by had his heart thudding hard in his chest. The gunmen were close. They needed to stay quiet and pray they'd keep moving.

Where they were was dark, though pinpricks of light filtered in from the top of the briars. He could see Charlie's eyes, large and clearly frightened they'd be caught. He reached over and squeezed her hand, trying to reassure her that he'd protect her at all costs.

The footfall moved away, and Bryan let out a relieved breath. They were going to stay put until he knew for sure it was safe to start moving again. He might have to change the plan and only travel at night. He had a compass and that could keep them going in the right direction. At least that way, it would make it harder for the drone tech and the kidnappers to spot them.

After a few minutes of listening and assured the abductors had moved farther down the mountain, Bryan removed his pack and opened the top zipper to retrieve two energy bars. He handed one to Charlie and peeled the wrapper from his.

She sighed and opened hers and took a bite, looking nervous. He couldn't blame her. The situation they were in was intense. These men were packing high-powered weaponry, and all he had was his Glock. He had fifteen rounds to work with, and their AR-15s could hold hundreds. Bryan was way outgunned and that's why he needed to be smart and strategic in every move he made.

Just then, he heard rocks sliding and a yelp and curse, one that brought a smile to his lips.

One thing was for sure, these men weren't used to the treacherous terrain, and that would give Bryan an advantage. He knew how to navigate through just about anything and hopefully that would get them off this mountain without any guns being fired.

****

It was hard for Charlie not to stare at the man so close to her. This was the first time, though seeing through the brushy vegetation was difficult, that she got to look at her rescuer. He was tall, his legs stretched out way beyond hers. His chest and arms were muscular, his chocolate-brown hair cut short, a hint of a wave on the top.

His features were sharp and angular yet appealing in all the right ways. His jaw was peppered with days' worth of growth, and it only made him more ruggedly handsome. She hadn't gotten close enough to see the color of his eyes, but they were fierce. He had tactical experience, clearly having spent a long time in the military like her father. She appreciated that he was accomplished like that. Only someone with his skill could get them out of this mess.

Charlie had only heard his voice a few times in hushed whispers, but it was deep and downright sexy. She could almost hear him talking dirty to her while making love, a thought that had her scolding herself for having it. They were in a life-or-death situation, and she was thinking about having sex with him. Warped in so many ways. *Cool your jets, Charlie. The man is risking his life to save yours. Have some respect.*

She nibbled on the energy bar he'd given her, trying

not to think about the fact that she needed to pee. She couldn't even remember the last time she had. Stuck there, when would she get the chance?

Charlie had to take her mind off her inflated bladder and try to figure out who ordered the drone instead. Someone who had it out for her father. She couldn't think of anyone who didn't love and respect him. So why use her to get him to comply to something?

Wait a minute. His reelection was coming up. Could his opponent be using her to get dirt on him? Right now, her dad was a shoo-in to win. Maybe a hit job would change that. Matthew Alsback was rich and powerful. Would he have the balls to go this far to win? It definitely was an avenue to explore once they were safely home. Until then, there wasn't much she could do, and that wasn't helping her mood. Idleness had never set well with Charlie. She'd always been a get up and go type of person. This being held thing had really set her off, and it made her angry. All she wanted to do was get the hell off this mountain and go back to her life. Was that even going to be possible if they didn't find who had hired these men that abducted her?

The man next to her shifted and brought her back to reality, and back to her full bladder. How was she going to get relief? It was going to get downright painful soon.

"Are you okay?" he asked in a low tone.

Should she tell him the truth? Charlie's face flushed with heat, sure her cheeks were now red.

"I really have to pee," she said, then looked away.

He reached into his bag and pulled out some strange bottle with a weird shaped top. "You can use this. I'll turn around."

"But…how—" Charlie trailed off, finally figuring

out how it worked. She paused at taking the gadget, not sure if she could even perform the action so close to him. He was virtually a stranger, and peeing had always been something she'd done alone. She was never one of those women who had to have company in the restroom.

"Don't suffer any longer than you have to, Charlie. I've been around female soldiers using one. I promise I won't peek."

Charlie believed him and she was going to use it. After all, bladder infections weren't pleasant and holding it could very likely cause one. She didn't need that.

With quick work of it, she took the gadget, did what she needed, then stretched out her arm out as far as she could to pour it out, feeling so much better.

Was there anything this man wasn't prepared to deal with? She didn't think so. At that moment she knew he'd get her to safety, and she was going to trust that.

Chapter 8

Bryan watched the last rays of daylight disappear and placed the backpack in place. Now that it was dark, they were going to start moving down the mountain again. He was going to have to keep one eye on the compass, the other on the trail itself, all the while avoiding the drone above. He prayed it didn't have heat sensors.

It was going to be treacherous traveling at night. The wrong move could be deadly. Rockslides were a real possibility, and he was going to have to make sure he and Charlie didn't cause one.

"Stay right behind me," he said in a tone just above a whisper. "Watch your step when we start the decline. One sure step at a time. Okay?"

She nodded, and they crawled out of the briars and stood. He reached for her hand and pulled her forward, slowly, since all they had for light was the moon above. Yes, he had a flashlight, but with the drone hovering somewhere, it wasn't safe to use one.

Inch by inch, Bryan moved down the mountain, watching his compass as they did. He didn't want to go in the wrong direction, not even for a minute. He knew the right coordinates and wouldn't stray for a second longer to get them to safety. Not when so much was at stake.

When he felt a rock start to slide, he caught himself,

and they stopped to find a safer route. This was going to be slow and tedious work. But there was no other way to get Charlie off this mountain. Every time he thought they were making progress, something came up to slow them down again. At this rate, it'd take them days to get to his vehicle. They'd need to find another hiding place to stay by morning. Bryan would have to locate one before any light came and that would be hard to do in the dark. What he wouldn't give for a pair of infrared glasses right now. Too bad he hadn't thought of that for his pack. It would have made this trek a hell of a lot easier.

He shook the thought and kept moving, all the while watching the time and compass. An hour before daylight, he started watching for a place to lay low for them until dark again.

A large rock formation came into view. He pointed to it, and the two headed that way.

Bryan reached the area and was surprised to see a cave of some sort, though it could house all kinds of dangerous critters. He'd need to scope out the inside before allowing Charlie to go anywhere near it.

"Stay here." He reached inside his pack and found the flashlight.

With caution, he stepped into the hole, relieved that there was no bear, the one thing he wasn't sure he could deal with. Bats, snakes and small animals were one thing; a momma brown was another.

He glanced around, not seeing anything other than spider webs that he quickly swiped away, then went back to get Charlie. They could hang out there until dark again. It seemed like a safe place as long as no one found them.

He ducked back out, took her hand and pulled her

inside, propping up the flashlight to illuminate the area.

Once they were both in the cave, he retrieved his thermal blanket and placed it on the ground, and signaled for her to sit, then got out two bottles of vitamin water and MREs. They might as well get something in themselves and then try and get some sleep. Bryan had been up for days, and it was going to start affecting his performance if he didn't get at least a few hours of rest. The light should keep critters from coming inside and those two abductors couldn't travel during the day, let alone at night, since they seemed to trip over their own feet. The drone wouldn't be able to spot them from above, so things should be okay for a while. At least that was his hope—the one thing they could utilize in this bad situation.

He grabbed the food and handed her one.

"Let's eat and try and get a few hours of sleep," he said, in his head, trying to calculate where they were in distance from his SUV. One more day should do it. That's if they didn't run into any trouble along the way.

Out here, that could be a high probability. He just needed to take it slow and steady and pray nothing catastrophic happened. All the while keeping Charlie from any bumps or bruises. Those men had done enough harm to her.

****

Charlie handed him her food and drink container and then laid back on the blanket, looking around at all the webs above. How many spiders were among them? She hated bugs and unfortunately, she was going to have to try and sleep with them around. The mere idea made her skin crawl.

The air inside the cave was cool and it caused

goosebumps. It felt like an icebox and the clothes she wore were not all that warm. *Try not to think about it.*

She rolled to her side, the rock wall flashing eerie shadows from the flashlight lighting up the cave. It was still better than in that room where they had kept her captive.

She shivered again and wrapped her arms around herself, hoping they'd keep her warm.

"Are you cold?"

His question caused her to turn and face him.

Big mistake. Even in this limited lighting, damned if the man wasn't the hottest specimen alive. He made her stomach do literal somersaults.

He reached into his bag and pulled out a package and unsealed it. It was a poncho-type raincoat, and he handed it to her. "That should help a little bit."

"Thank you." Charlie was grateful for this man's help. He clearly was prepared for anything, and that just made him sexier in her eyes—if that was even possible.

She quickly donned the coat and then laid down, flipping up the hood of the poncho to keep any critters away from her head of messy hair. She didn't need to pull a bug out days from now. The thought alone made her skin crawl again.

Her eyes grew heavy, and she nodded out only to be awakened when he touched her arm and whispered to stay very still. The flashlight had been turned off. Did that mean the men were close to catching them? Her heart started to thud painfully in her chest. She couldn't go back to that room. She'd go mad.

That's when she heard the hum of a four-wheeler close by. *Please don't find us.*

It had clearly stopped moving and was near them.

"Where the fuck are they?" the one who always came in the room said, his voice clogged with emotion. It was almost as if he feared for his life if they weren't found, and that made things even more dangerous.

"Let's keep going. They must be here somewhere." The four-wheeler revved up and started to move.

Charlie squeezed her eyes closed for a moment, then sighed and opened them, her heart rate easing a bit. That was damn close. How were they going to get free with these men having the four-wheeler and the weapons they carried? It seemed impossible, but then again, the man next to her appeared to be ready for anything. She needed to put her faith in him to get them out of this alive and free from these assholes.

She turned to him, wondering what was going on in that head of his. Was he as worried as she was? Nothing in his demeaner said as much. He looked as cool as a cucumber—something that eased her anxiety somewhat. If he wasn't concerned, she'd trust him to keep her safe.

He smiled, then laid back and placed his arm behind his head, appearing to not have a care in the world. Charlie needed to remember, he'd probably been in more dire situations and got through them. He could find a way to get them to safety as well.

Charlie lay next to him, the warmth of his body causing her own to heat. Damned if he wasn't a flame builder, one that quickly raced across her body.

She squeezed her eyes shut again, trying to get a semblance of control. They were in dire straits, and she was having impure thoughts about the man lying next to her. It was crazy and yet somehow exhilarating at the same time. Charlie hadn't really been all that head over heels about any guy in her life, too jaded from working with so many abused women. All the horror stories she'd heard and witnessed. Falling in love seemed almost dangerous to her. Who in their right mind wouldn't feel that way after seeing all these women and their children frightened by all these men who claimed to love them? It had seriously made her shy away from the male gender. And why she was pretend dating Sanderson.

When she met Emery, they'd struck up a deal to pretend to have a relationship to keep everyone at bay—it seemed like the perfect solution. He was always kind and considerate and they hung out when they both had the time. No strings attached and she liked that since she'd been trying to shake off a certain man who wouldn't leave her alone—a man old enough to be her father. Her dad would be so angry if he knew about the man's attention. That's why she never told him, afraid of what he'd do. Possibly something that would destroy his career. No way was she going to allow that.

Charlie had just dealt with it, though when the guy was in town, that wasn't always easy.

Chapter 9

Bryan woke, happy to see that the sun was going down. He needed to get Charlie off this damned mountain tonight. He'd checked to see where they were before falling back to sleep. They had about two miles to travel, and he knew if nothing unforeseen happened, they could get to his vehicle and on the road before sunset. He just needed to stay hyper-focused on not going too far off the path.

He gently nudged Charlie awake. "We need to get going. Do you need to relieve yourself or anything?"

She nodded, and he waited for her to do so at the mouth of the cave. When she stepped beside him, he gave her a reassuring smile, and they slowly moved out into the open. He glanced at his compass and started down an incline, each step careful and precise. If he slipped, Charlie surely would. He had to make sure the journey was safe for her first.

Two hours in, Bryan knew they were getting closer, and as long as the drone didn't spot them, he was sure they were going to make it to his SUV soon. The trail had gotten less steep, and that helped speed up the process.

Fifteen minutes led to a half hour, and Bryan spotted the path to the parking area of the park. They were so close now that he reached into his pockets for his keys. They were going to race to his vehicle and get the hell out of here and hope the drone wasn't around to spot them leaving.

They rounded a bend, and there it was. His SUV. When he got closer, he pressed the open-door button on his fob, and they both got in.

Bryan was going to wait to turn on the lights once he got closer to the highway. That drone was flying somewhere, and lights would only make it easy for the machine to spot them.

With ease, he backed up and took off, surprised to see at least four vehicles besides the one with the trailer in the lot. Were there people up on the mountain camping? Why hadn't they run across any of them? He'd think about that later. Now he just needed to get Charlie to Winding Creek and into their panic room to keep her in hiding until they found out who was behind this abduction.

Once they were on the road to the city, Bryan thought it was a good time to start asking Charlie some questions.

"I know that this is going to be hard, but we need to figure out who was behind all this. Who do you think would gain by blackmailing your father?"

She turned to him. "I've been thinking long and hard about this very question. Matthew Alsback is running against him in the primary, and my father is a shoo-in to win. Maybe this was all to get dirt on him in some way? Using congressional influence for self-gain could hurt him bad politically."

Bryan wasn't too sure of that anymore. People had done worse and kept their jobs in Congress. But it was a possibility for sure.

"Anyone else you could think of? Especially a

person who knew your whereabouts the night you were kidnapped?" Would she say anything about Sanderson or Nathan Beal?

Her eyes widened. "Sanderson knew I was at the Oasis that night, but would have no need to do such a thing. What would be his motive?"

"Maybe a bill he wants passed or doesn't? He is a rich man. Perhaps he feels as if he's not rich enough." Bryan had seen that type—military contractors whose greed made them willing to do just about anything to stay in power and rolling in dough.

"I really can't see that, but I can't tell you definitively that it wasn't him."

"Anyone else? Someone who cared enough to make sure you weren't abused while in captivity?"

"One of those men told me that they contacted my father. Couldn't we find out what was said in the conversation? That could help us figure out who orchestrated this."

Bryan would do that as soon as they got into cell phone range. Getting a ping on a location was one thing, but having service was another. He'd noted going in, when he lost signal, and they weren't there yet.

"I will do that as soon as we're in range to make a call. Up here are dead zones."

Suddenly, a stream of headlights from behind sent his heart into his throat. How the hell did they get to them this soon? He hadn't seen the drone. So, how were they spotted?

"Hang on. We're going to have to outrun these guys."

Bryan sped up, watching his rearview mirror, trying to gauge how far ahead he was from them.

Not far enough for sure. He'd have to outmaneuver them on the curves and try and get as far a lead as he could. Once they hit cell range, he'd contact his office and get some help. Until then, he'd use his combat training to stay in front of them.

A few hundred feet away was a winding area in the road. This is where he could lose them for a while. His driving skills were excellent, and he just needed theirs not to be. Maybe they'd even lose control and go off the road. Where they were, that could be deadly.

He took the first turn, his tire squealing in protest. The next was right behind, sharper and to the right, his wheels sliding on gravel on the side of the highway.

That was close, but he had to keep going and hope the men behind him would not be so lucky.

****

Charlie hung on for dear life, each sharp turn causing her heart to stop for a second as they made it to the next.

She silently prayed he wouldn't lose control and send them hurtling off into the deep ravine. Maybe it was better to close her eyes and hang on. Not to know how close they came to plunging to their deaths.

For sanity's sake, she thought it was.

Charlie squeezed her eyes closed and held on to the handle above the door. He was a capable man. She'd trust he could outwit these guys behind them and get them to safety. She just didn't want to watch him do so. Her heart couldn't take it.

Minutes into her self-protective action, she heard the tires sliding and she couldn't keep her eyes from opening, just in time to see them narrowly miss a tree, then noted they had straight road ahead of them. Thank

God. She glanced behind her. No lights were visible. Maybe they had run off the road.

A *ding. Ding. Ding*, made her look at her rescuer. "We're in cell service range now. I guess I got some texts." He sped up now that they were safe to do so.

He reached into his pocket and held out his phone. "Why don't you call your father. Find out what they were asking him to do to get you released. My passcode is zero, bravo, six, eight, three.

Charlie took his phone and punched in the code and pulled up the call app. She pressed in her dad's number and waited. It went to voicemail, and she left him a message.

"I had to leave a message." She handed him back the phone.

"Hopefully, he will call back soon. Until he does, we'll drive to Winding Creek and I'll place you in the office's safe room until we can find out who is behind all this."

"Why can't I go home?"

"You'll be safer at the office. No one would be able to get passed our security there."

All Charlie wanted to do was go home and crawl into her own bed, but that wasn't going to happen.

"Can you at least get some of my things. It's going to take me days to get my hair right, and I need my products to do that."

"Absolutely. Just make a list and I'll get anything you need."

It wasn't what she wanted, but she'd have to settle for now. Once her father learned of her freedom, he'd come to take her to his house, the home she grew up in. That would be much better in her eyes than another tiny room that would make her feel trapped and claustrophobic yet again.

In no time they were in Winding Creek, no signs of the car following them. In the city, they drove to a business area and then down into an underground parking area.

"Come on. Let's get you settled in. I'll stay with you until morning, and the others show up for work."

The two took the elevator up and then walked to the office where her hero opened the door with a keycard, entered an office area, and stepped into a room with a huge mahogany desk and floor-to-ceiling bookshelves. He touched something on one and the shelf moved, revealing a huge area inside. If this was where she was to stay, she could live with it. Everything inside sparkled and was surprisingly welcoming.

They stepped in, and he closed them inside. "Make yourself to home. Off to the right is a bedroom and full bath. There should be supplies you can use until I'm able to get to your place to pick up your things. There is military tees and boxers you can sleep in for tonight. While you get cleaned up, I'll scrounge us up something to eat."

"Before I go, can I get your name? I'm sorry it took this long to ask."

"Bryan Gamble."

"You saved my life, Bryan. I can't thank you enough."

He shrugged. "It's what I get paid for."

"Still. I do appreciate everything you did." With that, Charlie turned and went to the bedroom. She was going to take a long shower and hoped she would never experience what she had these last few days ever again.

Chapter 10

Bryan walked over to the kitchen area and glanced in the fridge, shocked at how stocked it was. Had they expected them, or was this prepped every few days for the just-in-case scenarios? Then again, everyone who worked at Bolton was ex-military and knew the drill of always being prepared for anything.

He inhaled a deep breath, suddenly feeling weary. Now that they were safe, he could finally relax, though did he know how to do that? Not really. He'd been constantly moving since he joined the military, and even when he retired, he'd kept a grueling pace. He was never a sit-still kind of person. Staying busy quieted his overactive mind. He wouldn't even know what to do with himself if he didn't keep going forward.

He pulled out everything he'd need to make them a veggie omelet and started to chop mushrooms, red peppers and onions.

He found a large skillet and some olive oil and turned on a burner, sautéing the vegetables first. When he had the omelet ready, he placed it in the oven to keep warm while he went to the separate bathroom to get cleaned up. In his go bag he had extra clothes, and he couldn't wait to feel clean again. It had been days since he'd had a shower, and he needed one to help him wind down.

Under the jets, he let the water course over him for

a few minutes, then grabbed the bodywash and cleaned himself, feeling the fatigue set in.

Once they ate, he was going to send Charlie off to bed and get some sleep.

Bryan finished his shower, turned off the water, and dried himself. He dressed and turned to the outer room, surprised to see Charlie sitting on the couch, working a wide-toothed comb through her wet hair.

"Are you hungry?" he asked, stepped over to the stove to pull out the eggs.

"Starving, actually."

He retrieved some plates, then glasses he filled with orange juice.

Both seated, she asked, "Did my dad ever call back?"

"Not yet, but then again, it is the middle of the night. He was probably sleeping and hasn't checked his voicemail yet. When Vince gets into the office, I'll have him call your father to tell him we have you here."

Bryan took a bite of his food, happy to have a warm meal. She gobbled down hers and then drank her juice, yawning after she did.

He got up and rinsed the dishes, and placed them into the dishwasher. "I think we should try and get a few hours of sleep. Outside this room, Vince will have been notified that we are inside and will need to speak with us. So, let's get a little rest before that happens."

She nodded, rose and headed for the bedroom. Before she entered the room, she turned. "Thank you, Bryan. I'd probably be back in those guys' hands if you hadn't come to rescue me."

"Like I told you. That's what I get paid for. I'm just glad you are safe."

She smiled, then stepped into the room and closed the door.

Bryan cleared his throat and went in search of a blanket and pillow. He found both in a cabinet and then walked to the couch. He was so tired. He hoped he'd be able to sleep.

****

Voices woke Charlie from a sound sleep. She had no idea what time it was, but she needed to get up and find out if her father had been called and told she was here. She wanted him to take her home where she could feel safe, not that Bryan hadn't done that the minute they reached the safe room, especially since no one but Bolton Security could get to them. But she wanted her father, a man who had always made her life secure.

Besides, Bryan was too distracting. She couldn't seem to think straight with him around. She thought fanciful things that were stupid. The one thing she'd promised herself growing up was to never fall for a military man. She'd seen firsthand how country came first. Even after they left the armed forces. They were duty-bound to serve, and it was ingrained for a lifetime. She wanted more than that in the man she loved. No matter how damned good-looking they were. So, it was best to get away from this gorgeous creature before he changed her mind. For some reason, she knew that wouldn't be easy with him. He exuded masculinity and looked every bit as good as any GQ model around—a lethal combination in her eyes.

Charlie watched her own mother worry day after day when her father was in harm's way. Why would she want to subject herself to that? She wouldn't. So, it was best to steer clear of Bryan.

She rose and walked to the door, not recognizing the voice other than Bryan's. It wasn't her father.

She stepped out the door and glanced at Bryan, then the other man standing next to him. Clearly, ex-military as well, his hair cut short, a cluster of gray strands in his sideburns. Handsome in his own right, with hawk-like features, his eyes a lighter shade of blue, almost gray from this distance.

"Ms. Reed." The man walked toward her. "I'm Vince Samuels. I can't tell you how relieved I am to see you."

She gave him a weak smile. "Have you talked to my father yet?"

"I haven't gotten a hold of him, no. I've left messages. He hadn't returned my calls."

Charlie thought that was strange since he'd contracted them to find her. What could it mean? Was he out of cell range somewhere? That didn't make sense with all this happening. He would have stayed close to his phone. Something didn't feel right.

"Something's wrong. My father would have been here the minute he learned I was safe."

The older man nodded. "I was thinking the same. But I'm not sure what to do."

"We need to go to his home and see if he's there."

Bryan shook his head. "*We* are not going anywhere. I'll go and check myself."

Charlie knew he was trying to protect her, but she'd be the only one to know if anything there was out of place. He wouldn't. She needed to go, and she wasn't taking no for an answer, no matter how many times he refused to take her.

"I'm going with or without you," she said in a tone

he'd better listen to.

"Your father would be angry at putting you in harm's way again."

"Then don't."

He stared at her for the longest time. Charlie wasn't going to budge. He was taking her with him no matter what. He might as well be reserved to that now.

"Okay. Let me get you something to wear, and we will go."

She'd almost forgotten she was in a military t-shirt and skivvies.

He walked to a utility closet and rifled through items and came back and handed her a pair of fatigues.

Charlie ran to quickly change. They needed to hurry. What if something happened—what if her father was lying on the floor at his home as they waited for him to return their calls? They had to get there, and they needed to do it immediately.

Chapter 11

Bryan turned to Charlie once they were on the road. "Your father does have security, right?"

"Not unless he's in Washington. He believes he can take care of himself at home since he's ex-military."

"And his staff are okay with this?"

"Try and dissuade my father when he sets his mind to something. He won't listen, believe me. I've tried talking to him about this."

"How about you, Charlie? Weren't you supposed to have security yourself? Apparently, the stubborn apple doesn't fall far from the tree."

"No one had ever bothered me until now. Never even had an angry e-mail. Why would I need a bodyguard?"

"If you had people by your side, they never would have grabbed you outside the Oasis."

"I guess, but all these years I'd never had a problem until four days ago. This was about my father, not me."

"But that isn't entirely true. Didn't Leon Sherman threaten you?" Bryan did understand her need to live a normal life. After all, she had until her father was elected to Congress six years ago.

"He was just angry. Said things to strike back. Oh, take a left on Cambridge." Her directions drew him back to the mission, getting to her father's and finding out why he wasn't returning any calls.

He took the turn and entered an upscale area where the homes were in the millions of dollars range. Bryan could never in his lifetime own one. How had Congressman Reed done so on an ex-military salary, or a congressman for that matter?

"Did your father come from money?"

"No, but my mother did. Her family owns Arber Publications."

The oldest and most prestigious newspaper in Boulder, which was still successful even in the digital age. Now, he could understand how Dennis Reed could live here and why Charlie had that condo in a ritzy part of town.

"Turn right here." She pointed to Cranberry Street. "Number twelve is my dad's house."

Bryan pulled up the driveway, taking in the three-story, red-brick home. White columns lined the right and left side of the door, topiaries sat next to them adding color.

Charlie rushed to get out of his vehicle and raced to the door. She tried to open it but found it locked. That didn't faze her. She dug through one of the plants and found a gray rock, sliding the bottom open to reveal a key inside.

Moments later, they were both in the house, Charlie calling out for her father. When no one answered, she took off toward the staircase. "You do the downstairs, I'll search the second floor," she said racing up the steps.

Bryan wasn't sure it was wise for them to separate, but she wasn't going to stop. He'd search the lower level quickly, then race to get to her. He went from room to room, noting things that might indicate that someone had been there recently. Dishes were in the sink, leftover food still sitting on the table. Was Dennis the type of person to just leave a mess like this? He'd need to ask Charlie. Off the kitchen was a utility room where there was a door leading to the back yard. He reached the knob and found it unlocked. That's when he noticed some blood droplets on the marble flooring. Had someone gotten to Dennis through this door and dragged him out? This was not looking good, and he'd need to call Vince and let him know what he'd found.

Before he could reach for his phone, Charlie came into the room, her eyes filled with tears. "I couldn't find him, and his room was a mess. Drawers in his dresser open, the bed unmade."

Bryan wasn't sure if he should point out the blood or not. It didn't look fresh. Telling her would probably scare her even more.

"This door was unlocked. If someone did get to him, this is how they got in. Did you notice the food out on the table and the dishes in the sink? Would he have done that?"

"No! He's ex-military, remember? He would have never left the house like this on purpose. Someone forced him to leave. Do you think they grabbed him because I escaped? Is this my fault?"

"Of course not. They want him to do something for them, and it must be because of him being a congressman. We need to find out what his schedule is for the next week or so. That could be a key to why you and he now, were taken."

****

Charlie's heart literally hurt. Her escaping had caused her father's abduction, and that made her feel terrible. If she'd simply stayed put and waited, this wouldn't have happened. Then again, she could now be missing a finger or two if she had.

Still, her father was missing, and it was her fault.

"Who would know your father's work schedule? Is there one person who would have that?" Bryan's question pulled her out of her recrimination.

"Roy Ames, his chief of staff. He'd have all that information."

"Do you have a way of getting a hold of him? A personal number perhaps?"

"Usually, I call my father directly, but I can call Dad's congressional office. Then an aide can have Roy get back to me. Hang on. Dad has all relevant numbers in his office. I can call him from there. We will need to wait here until he returns the call or gives them another number. It's up to you? Maybe Dad has a calendar with his upcoming committee events as well in his office."

"Let's go look."

Charlie led the way to her father's office, a room he'd spent a lot of time in when he was home—one she wasn't allowed to enter while he was working. Even when her mother was alive, she didn't go in if the door was closed.

She reached the entrance and took a long breath, feeling almost apprehensive about going inside. This was her father's private domain, and she felt guilty entering it.

Shaking her anxiety, she turned the knob and opened the door, her father's scent instantly bombarding her. He'd been here recently.

Charlie stepped over to his desk, his laptop sitting open on top. Weird that it wasn't shut unless whoever took him surprised him while he was working. Could be where he was last and why his cologne was so strong. All his info was on his computer. Too bad she didn't know his password. It was probably thumb or face-activated since he was a US congressman on important committees. Everything had to be encrypted and kept safe.

Right now, she'd just go through his desk. She grabbed the handle of a side drawer and was shocked that it was locked. Why would he lock his drawers in his office unless he was worried that someone would look inside? What would he keep in them that he needed to hide?

She glanced over at Bryan and frowned. "For some reason, his desk is locked?"

"We may need to pry it open. He'll understand since we are trying to find him." He grabbed the letter opener in a circular container on top of his desk, then worked at the lock on the large middle drawer. It only took him moments to get it to pop free. He opened it, graphic pictures inside making Charlie gasp.

No way was she seeing these. Bryan cleared his throat, and she glanced at him, her eyes filling with tears. Her father was engaging in a sexual act with someone who looked younger than herself. Who took the photos, and was he being blackmailed in some way because of them? But if that were the case, why kidnap her and then him? She had so many questions, and the only one who could answer them was missing.

Chapter 12

Bryan could tell Charlie was shocked by the pictures in the drawer, which meant she hadn't known about the young woman in them. What should he say, if anything? Maybe it was best to pretend to have not seen them? But it was yet another avenue to follow. They needed to know who the woman was and if she could have a connection to Charlie and her father's abduction.

Perhaps something else inside his desk could reveal that. He opened a side drawer and found a small book inside and leafed through it, finding a series of passwords to different accounts, one catching his eye—a gentleman's fetish-type online club. So, Dennis had membership to a place that catered exclusively to a man's S & M desires. At least he wasn't married. Something like this could ruin his career, though, everything seemed to go nowadays. You could get away with activities that once ended your career. But this led to the seedier side of society and could've brought the wrong type of people into his life, and could be how Charlie was kidnapped. Once she escaped, they came directly for Dennis.

It was a possibility that Bryan would need to follow up on. Hopefully, he could find something in his computer now that he had his password.

He quickly found and typed in the sequence, then found his email and glanced through dozens of unopened ones. Nothing that looked odd or suspicious until he saw one that had been opened this morning at six AM. So, was it Dennis who opened the mail or did someone else? It was from an Amanda Dillion. Bryan reopened it and read; a sick feeling left in the pit of his stomach. It had a picture—a sonogram photo to be precise. This woman was pregnant and was insinuating that it was the congressman's child.

He glanced over his shoulder and saw Charlie's eyes welling with tears. What a way to find out you were going to have a sibling. It had to be a shock, to say the least. Maybe Dennis wasn't kidnapped, though why the mess and the dried blood?

They needed to find this woman who sent the email and talk to her. Make sure he wasn't with her at that moment.

He reached for his phone and called Sterling.

"What do you need, Bryan?"

"I want you to find an address for an Amanda Dillion and anything else about her. Charlie's father is missing, and this woman had a secret relationship with him."

"I'll call you back with an address."

Bryan ended the call and turned to Charlie. "Let's look for your dad's aide's number and call and find out his schedule. Hopefully, Sterling will have this woman's address by then, and we can go talk to her."

Charlie rifled around in his desk and then pulled out a slip of paper and picked up the phone on the desk, and punched in the number. "Hello," she said once someone picked up. "This is Dennis's daughter, Charlene. Is Roy around? I need to know my dad's schedule for the next week."

"He was called away for some type of emergency. When he gets back, I can have him call you."

"All right, but could you call me on my friend's phone? I'm leaving my father's house now."

Bryan relayed his cell phone number to her to give them, and she ended the call just as Bryan's phone rang.

"What do you have?"

"I found two. One is a fifty-year-old and the other, twenty-five. Which one do you want?"

"Give me the twenty-five-year-old's."

"She lives in a gated community off Willard Drive, 5673 Ansine. I'll do a background on her and call you back in a few hours."

"Thanks." Bryan glanced at Charlie, who looked almost green now.

"Are you okay?"

"Just swimming. How often does someone my age find out I'm about to be an older sister?"

"You'd probably be surprised."

She gave him a slight smile.

"Let's go see what this woman has to say, then we'll go from there."

Bryan led Charlie from the home, making sure the doors were locked before leaving.

In the car, he put the address into the navigation and pulled out from the driveway. How would he feel in Charlie's shoes? His own father might have been a drunk, but as far as he knew, he never cheated on his mother, though if he had, and they had separated, maybe she'd be alive today.

****

Charlie took in a long breath as she stared at the home this woman lived in. It was nice for someone her age. Did her father help pay for it? That was the million-dollar question. One she intended to find out.

She let Bryan knock on the door, still trying to digest what was happening. She was about to meet a woman who was her age and was sleeping with her father.

The door opened and her jaw slacked, the blonde standing there looking frightened. What was she scared of?

“Are you Amanda Dillion?” Bryan’s inquiry drew Charlie back to him.

“Yes. What is this about?”

“Dennis Reed.”

Her face paled. Why?

“Has something happened to him?”

Charlie stepped in front of Bryan. “Do you know who I am?”

The blonde took a step back, her eyes narrowing. “Should I?” Charlie couldn’t believe this woman was sleeping with and about to have a child with her father, and she didn’t know he had a daughter. “I’m his daughter,” she spat out, more than angry with her dad for not telling her what was going on in his life.

She frowned. “No. He has a son named Charlie.”

“I’m Charlene/Charlie.”

“Dennis never shared much of his life with me. I just assumed it was because he was a congressman. All he said was he had a child named Charlie.”

“How did you two meet?” Bryan asked.

“At a fundraising event for Dennis that Nathan Beal held at Bayberry country club. I served drinks and food for the caterer I worked part-time for.”

Bryan turned to Charlie, clearly recognizing the name. How? Then again, who didn’t know Nathan in

Colorado? The man was well known in political circles and had tried to get her to go out with him, even knowing how her father would feel about it. He'd wrote all these flowery letters that only made him look pathetic in her eyes. She wondered if Bryan had found them by the look he gave her. Surely, he wouldn't think the two were having an affair. Charlie had seen too many couples end a loving relationship and turn it into something unrecognizable. That's why she had a fake relationship with Sanderson. It was easy and wouldn't lead to someone ending up being beaten half to death. She'd seen too much of that working at her non-profit.

She shook the thought and took a breath. "Have you seen my father today?"

The blonde shook her head. "I haven't seen Dennis in weeks. He told me this wasn't working for him. That I needed to find someone my own age and settle down. Of course, that was before I found out I'm pregnant. I sent him an email last night with a sonogram picture. He never got back to me. I guess he doesn't care."

"He's missing." For whatever reason, Charlie needed to defend her father.

"Since when?"

"I don't know how long he's been missing. Someone opened your email. That's how we found you."

The woman frowned. "Could it have been him who opened it?"

Charlie nodded. "Like I said, I have no clue what happened, only that he's missing."

"This may be a bit personal," Bryan interjected. "But did you know that Dennis was a part of an online gentleman's group? Was into some bondage type stuff?"

"What? No. I don't believe that."

"There was a picture that was in Dennis's desk that seemed pretty S and M. The woman in the picture looked like you."

"No. Not me. Are you sure it wasn't one of those deepfake pictures? Maybe someone was trying to blackmail Dennis."

Charlie looked at Bryan. "I hadn't even thought of that. That could be a possibility."

"So, when are you due?" Charlie asked, suddenly wanting to know when she'd have a half sister or brother.

"In six months. Will you keep me posted when you find Dennis? He might have ended things, but I still love him."

Charlie suddenly felt bad for her. She knew her father wouldn't abandon the child, but Amanda didn't know that. "Give me your number and I'll call you when we find him."

The blonde left, then returned with a slip of paper. "This has both my cell phone and land line. Please let me know as soon as you can." She handed Charlie the paper and then closed the door.

Bryan took a hold of her hand, and a tingle raced up her arm. "Are you okay?"

"Yes. I just wish Dad would have told me he was seeing someone."

"How well would you have taken that knowing the woman was your age?"

That was a good question. One she didn't know the answer to. The whole thing had her head whirling. One way or another, she was going to have to resign herself to knowing she was going to have a sibling, and there wasn't any way around that.

Chapter 13

"What we need to do is go back to your father's house so I can get Sterling, my tech guy, to look at the picture in his desk to analyze if it has been doctored in some way. Also, check to see if he got any phone calls while we were gone."

"Can we stay there tonight just in case he comes home?"

Bryan didn't see why not. They could set the alarm and make sure all the doors were locked and bolted. "Sure. Is there anything you need at your place?"

"I'd love to get a few things if you think that'd be alright."

"That'll be fine." He punched her address into his navigational system.

"I take it you've been at my place when those men held me captive?"

"I was, yes."

She looked almost embarrassed by the fact, why he hadn't a clue.

"Don't worry. I didn't rummage around your underwear drawer."

That earned him a smile. "Good to know."

"I did notice that your place is very clean."

"That was my mother's influence. She was very tidy."

"When did you lose her?"

She inhaled and released the breath. “I was almost fifteen. I still miss her.”

“I lost mine a while back, too. She was always working, so I never really saw much of her.”

“What about your dad? Is he still around?”

“Unfortunately, yes.”

Her eyes widened. “Not a fan?”

“Not in the least. He was an alcoholic and a lazy bastard. My mother supported us. When she died, he found a new woman to pick up the slack.”

“Is that why you entered the military? To get away?”

Bryan glanced at her for a moment. “Yes.”

“How long did you serve?”

“Fifteen years.”

“Five more and you could have retired with a military pension.”

“I know, but I had some friends get killed, and it sort of made up my mind for me to get out.”

“I’m so sorry. Were you there at the time it happened?”

He cleared his throat. “Yeah. I still have a hard time sleeping.”

She squeezed his arm, and a ripple of sexual awareness hit him hard in the groin. There was something about Charlie that he was drawn to, but she was a client’s daughter and off-limits.

Bryan made the turn into her gated community and found the key card to insert into the gate, and the arm rose. He drove forward and took the turn onto her street, pulling up into the driveway.

They exited the vehicle. “Let me go first just in case.”

He dug the house key out of his pocket and inserted

it into the lock. Inside, he went straight to the alarm box and punched in the code.

He glanced around, seeing no evidence of any kind of break-in. "Come on in, Charlie," he called, and waited for her to enter and close the door.

"Let's get what you need and get back to your dad's."

"It should only take me a few minutes. I'll be right back." Bryan watched her walk away, thinking no one looked so good in military fatigues. One thing was for sure, Charlie had a grade-A behind.

He shoved the thought away and took out his phone. It might be a good idea to call Vince and let him know that Dennis was missing. Sterling couldn't even track Dennis's phone since it was sitting on the kitchen table at his home.

He scrolled through his contacts and found his info and pressed call. Instead of Vince, Nina answered. "Hey, Nin, is Vince around? We went to Dennis's and found his back door unlocked, dried blood on the kitchen floor and Dennis missing. I thought I should let Vince know that Charlie and I plan to stay at her father's house in case he returns. If he needs anything, just tell him to call me."

"This is definitely not a good outcome," she said, her voice now strained. "We need to find out why he and his daughter were targeted. They want something and we need to know what that is."

"I'll try to learn what I can on my end. It had to have something to do with his position in Congress. What else could it be?"

"I'll have Sterling do a deep dive on Dennis. Maybe he was keeping something from us."

"Tell Sterling to call me after you talk to him. I want to send him a picture I want analyzed for any changes to the photo."

"You think it may have been doctored?"

"Yes. Like I said, things have gone from bad to worse, and we need to find who might have taken Dennis and why."

****

Charlie carried her bag into her old room, having left Bryan downstairs on the phone with one of his colleagues. She placed the overnight bag on her bed and took a long, cleansing breath. This room had always been her haven. Now, it felt cold and empty.

How much had her father kept from her since she left home? This young woman was bad enough, but she was starting to wonder if he was caught up in something nefarious and couldn't find a way out—that had been the reason for her kidnapping and then his own.

She shook her head. *No.* Her father was a good man. There was more to this, and hopefully Bryan and his crew could get to the bottom of it before her dad ended up dead.

Right now, she was going to shower and change. Then she'd go down and see if Bryan had learned something.

In the shower, she reached for her bath products and washed her hair, then used her detangler to work out the mats.

It would take days to get her strands the way they'd been before her abduction, but this was a start.

Once clean, she stepped out and dried off, returning to her bedroom to get dressed.

A knock made her jump half out of her skin. She

grabbed her robe and threw it around her while going to the door to open it.

Bryan's eyes widened, only making her self-conscious.

"I wanted to update you on what we've learned."

"Okay." Charlie was not at all sure she wanted to hear it by the look on his face.

"The photo was indeed doctored. Your father knew, I'm sure, but was probably concerned that if released, it'd taint his career."

"I'm sure it would. Poor widower caught in a bondage situation. Who would vote for him after that?"

"Again, in today's politics, you'd be surprised. What used to tank a career ten years ago no longer applies. We now have sexual predators walking the halls of Congress."

Charlie lived in a sheltered world. All this seemed like a game-changer to her, but to Bryan, not so much. Then again, he had more worldly experience than she did. He was probably right.

"I wanted to also ask if you knew a man by the name of Lukas Moorhouse? He was seen with your father two days ago going into Harlan Community Bank on Midway. Sterling used recognition software to find the footage. Does your dad bank there?"

Charlie had no clue. "Sorry. I don't know where my father banks or who this man is."

"That's okay. We are looking into it as we speak. When you get dressed, come on down. I thought we'd order some takeout and wait for Sterling to call back. Oh, also we need to access your father's voicemail. In case there is something there."

"All right. I'll be down in a few minutes."

Charlie threw on a pair of cream-colored cashmere pants and a matching top, along with dark blue cardigan. The temps were dipping down into the thirties at night, and this would keep her warm.

She stepped out of her room, alerted to Bryan talking to someone. Downstairs, she was surprised to see Vince, who she'd met earlier that day, standing just inside the door.

When he saw her, he stopped talking. Why? Was it bad news. Had they found her father dead? The mere thought caused her body to grow cold, making her shake.

Before she could ask, Vince shook Bryan's hand and left, only triggering goose bumps to erupt all over her.

"What?" She tensed, afraid to hear what he was going to tell her.

"Calm down. As far as we know, your father is still alive."

Charlie released a staggering breath. "So, then what did he learn that had both of you looking so distraught?"

"Lukas Moorhouse was found dead an hour ago in his home west of town, and as far as we know, your father was the last person to see him alive."

Chapter 14

Bryan sat across from Charlie at the kitchen table, still running over what he'd learned in his head. When he had first left Charlie upstairs, his body had experienced a haywired electrical current at seeing her still wet and her robe clinging to her naked body beneath. Jesus, mother, and Mary, she was exquisite. She had managed to tame her hair, and she took his breath away.

Thank God Vince had showed up to extinguish the smoldering flames. Learning that this Moorhouse man had been found with a gunshot to the head had cooled his ardor instantly. According to Vince, it had looked like a suicide, but was it or had someone staged it to look like one? Unfortunately, there was no way to find out without access to the scene and no way the local PD would give them that.

Bryan took a bite of his food and watched Charlie nibble at her own. If she hadn't seen him and Vince talking, he wouldn't have told her about this guy's death. But she came down and knew something was wrong, and he couldn't lie to her. She'd see through that.

"You aren't eating. Don't you like it?"

"It's fine. I'm just worried about my father. You don't think he was somehow the catalyst to this Moorhouse's death, do you?"

"I really don't know, Charlie, but you can be sure that we will find out. Before Vince showed up, I found your dad's PIN to his voicemail. We can listen to them while we eat, and you can tell me if you know the caller or not. Can you do that?"

She nodded.

Bryan grabbed the man's phone and entered his PIN into the voicemail app and waited.

"Dennis, why haven't you returned my call? It's urgent that I speak to you today."

Bryan looked at Charlie, who said, "That's Roy, his chief of staff. He still hasn't returned my call. That's uncharacteristic of him. Something is seriously wrong with all of this."

"Let's go on to the next voicemail."

"Why aren't you getting back to me, Dennis? You know how important what we are working on is."

"Do you have any idea what the two were referring to here?" Bryan asked, wondering if this was key to why Dennis was abducted and Moorhouse was dead.

"I don't. Dad and I never discussed any of his work on committees. It was unethical and my father was a stickler for congressional decorum."

"All right. Let's move on."

He played the next voicemail. *"If you don't get back to me within the hour, everything we have worked toward with be flushed down the toilet."*

Bryan rubbed at his stubbled chin. "We are going to need to talk to him. This might be key to finding out why your father was taken. Maybe to stop whatever the two were working on."

"What else can I do? I tried to get him to call me. It's not like we can tell him Dad's missing in a voicemail. Everyone would find out."

Charlie was right. They were going to have to wait

and hope the man called. Until then, they would find out more about this Moorhouse character. He was involved in some way and possibly murdered because of it.

"Tomorrow, we will investigate Moorhouse and how he might be linked to your father. Perhaps there is something there to indicate what Dennis was working on. Right now, you and I need to eat and get some sleep. Until morning, there is nothing else we can do. Roy may be waiting to call you back. It's late, and calling at this time might go against what the man was taught. Who knows, but we will worry about it in the morning. Now eat. You need to regain your strength. You will need it. Hopefully, we'll learn everything we need to tomorrow."

Yes, Bryan was trying to appease her, but she had to calm down. This worrying would only cause her to crash, and they didn't need that going forward.

****

Charlie had started to doze off when she heard a loud crash coming from below her. It couldn't be Bryan since he was in the room across from her unless he'd gone back down after she got into bed.

Maybe it was her father?

She rushed to pull her arms through her robe and raced out the door right as Bryan was coming from the guest bedroom, shirtless, zipping and buttoning his pants. If she had time, she would have loved to take a moment to admire the man's perfect physique, but someone was in the house—a person who knew the alarm code, otherwise, it would have gone off.

"You need to stay here," he whispered to her.

"No. It could be Daddy. I'm going with you." Yes, Charlie could be putting them both at risk, but she didn't care. She was going, and he wasn't stopping her.

He looked as if he wanted to argue, but instead started for the stairs, indicating she stay behind him. She could do that.

They slowly took the steps down to the ground floor, hesitating on the landing to glance around. A noise alerted them that someone was in her father's office.

They moved toward the open door, every cell in Charlie's body firing on all cylinders. She prayed it was her father inside.

The light on his desk illuminated the room in a soft glow. Bryan took a step into the office, and she followed.

The intruder sat at her father's desk, his laptop open and on by the light emanating around it. Charlie recognized who it was right away.

"Roy, what are you doing here?" she shouted, not thinking what would happen if he was there for nefarious reasons.

The man looked up, clearly surprised by their presence.

"Answer her." Bryan's tone sent chills erupting over Charlie's body. This was the soldier he'd been, one with a killer instinct. She had seen it in her father, too. It was ingrained in military personnel, and it never left even after leaving the service.

"I'm here trying to find something in your father's files. I've been trying to call him for two days. I finally decided to jump on a plane, hoping to find him home. I need the documents he and I have been gathering for the last six months. If I don't find them, we are all going to be in a world of hurt."

"How did you get into the house and deactivate the alarm system?" Bryan asked.

"As chief of staff, I have all that information, and I

have a spare key to this house."

"Why didn't you return my call?" Charlie asked, wondering if she could believe a word he was saying. Her father never said anything about Roy having a key to the house. Then again, why would he, since she no longer lived there?

"I didn't get any message that you called. Who did you talk to?"

Charlie hadn't even asked. "I don't know."

"In the morning, I'll call the congressional office and find out."

"What were you and Daddy working on that was so urgent?"

"Sorry, that's privileged."

Of course it was.

Ever since her father took office years ago, he had kept everything work related to himself. To the point of it being annoying to Charlie, especially since he worked more hours than not. She'd become an afterthought in his life, and probably why he'd tried to make up for that by buying her things that he thought would bring her joy. It also fed her now shopping addiction—the one thing she didn't like about herself. She worked a job that had her dealing with women with nothing after leaving their husbands, and she had a condo full of stuff she didn't need. It made her feel guilty most days. It was something she needed to work on after this nightmare was over.

"Did you find what you needed?" Bryan asked Roy, bringing her back to the present.

"No. It's not here. Where is your father?"

"He's missing? We found the back door unlocked. His phone was on the table. We think someone took him."

Roy's eyes widened, and he shook his head. "I told him not to tell anyone what we were working on. He must have said something to someone. Shit."

"How bad is this?" Bryan asked.

"Let's just say on a scale of one to ten, it's one hundred."

Chapter 15

Bryan woke, confused as to where he was until he remembered he was sleeping in a guest room at Dennis's house. They'd decided to go to bed, Roy taking Dennis's room on the ground floor. Not knowing what he was hiding had Bryan's stomach in knots, especially after learning it was high-level bad. This was the key to finding Dennis, but Roy refused to say any more. They were going to have to do everything the hard way—learn it on their own. But how?

He shoved the covers aside and quickly made up the bed. The military had taught him well. This was something he never stopped doing, even if he was in a hurry.

At the foot of the bed was a seat where he'd placed his bag. He found a change of clothes and stepped into the guest bathroom to shower.

This was another thing he learned to do efficiently. Quick and squeaky clean, and then he dressed and went down to the main floor, where he could smell coffee brewing. He'd probably need at least half a pot after the night he'd had.

In the kitchen, Bryan found Charlie and Roy sitting at the table, in a conversation that stopped the minute they saw him.

"Good morning." He made his way to the coffeemaker to grab a cup and filled it to the rim. "How long have you two been up?"

"Not long." Charlie glanced back at Roy to reiterate that. Something was up with the two, but it looked like neither was going to say anything. Bryan just hoped it wasn't something he needed to know.

"When do the congressional offices open? We need to find out who didn't relay Charlie's message to you."

"I texted my secretary last night about this. She said that somehow Latten, our intern, lost the message."

Bryan frowned. "And you believe her?"

"Why would she lie?"

"Why indeed. How long has this Latten worked for you?"

"Just a short while. Why does that matter?"

"I'm simply asking." Bryan had a whirl of questions running around in his head. First and foremost, did this Latten deliberately lose Charlie's message, or was she/he that incompetent?

"Today, we need to find out how your father was connected to the man who was found dead and why both he and your dad were at the bank three days ago."

"How do we do that?"

"My people are working on the background of Moorhouse. I think as your father's daughter, maybe we can go to this bank and find out what he came in for that day."

"Okay. Let me run up and get my purse and coat, and we can get started on that right now."

Once Charlie was gone, Bryan turned his attention to Roy. "What was going on with you two when I came in? It's important not to hide anything that would help us find Dennis."

"It wasn't anything that would do that. It was

something private. Something you don't need to know."

Bryan picked up on the condescending tone of this man's voice and was instantly annoyed. Did Roy think he was just some grunt—didn't deserve to know anything about Charlie and Dennis's life?

Charlie stepped back into the kitchen, and Bryan thought it best to just leave. Hopefully, by the time they returned, they'd at least know why Dennis and Moorhouse had gone to the bank. If money was exchanged, then they'd need to find out how much and why. Though, how they would learn those facts with the man dead was going to be a problem.

****

Charlie allowed Bryan to open the bank door for her and followed behind, his hand lingering on the small of her back. The gesture caused a charge to zip down to her toes. What was it about this man that caused her body to respond to his slightest touch?

At the desk, she smiled at the lovely blonde. "Can we see your branch manager?" They had to learn what her father had come there for days ago.

"Can I say what it's about?"

"It's pertaining to my father, Congressman Dennis Reed."

Her hazel eyes widened, clearly recognizing the name.

"I'll see if he's available."

Charlie glanced back at Bryan and was struck by how sigh-worthy his face was. He might be ex-military but she found herself attracted to him more than she'd ever been to anyone before. Just being around him made her knees feel weak and caused a rash of goose bumps to erupt all over her body.

"Mr. Travis will see you. Follow me."

Keep your focus, Charlie. No more going into romantic entanglement mode.

They entered an office and were indicated to take a seat.

"What can we do for you, Ms. Reed?"

"My father was in here a few days ago. Is it possible to find out why?"

"Can't you ask your father?"

"He's busy in Washington, D.C. right now."

The older man's expression changed from friendly to suspicious. "Can I see some ID?"

"Of course." Charlie reached into her handbag and pulled out her wallet, and extracted her license. She then handed it to him.

He punched something into his computer and then returned his attention to her. "So, your father did make you his contact and beneficiary on any and all of his accounts. Now, what did you need?"

"Can you tell me what he did when he came in last?"

Again, he glanced at his computer and said, "He accessed his safety deposit box."

"Can I go see what's inside it?"

"According to this, yes. You have access."

"Let me get the spare key he left for you, and we will step into the vault."

The man left and Charlie turned to Bryan. "You probably won't be allowed inside. What do you want me to do?"

"Use my phone and take a picture of everything that is inside." He handed it to her.

"Ms. Reed. Follow me," the bank Manager said. "Your friend can wait in the lobby."

Charlie trailed the man to the back and into a vault filled with boxes. He inserted both keys into box sixty-five and then pulled out the long box inside. “I’ll leave you to look. When you are finished, just place the box back into the slot and close the door. It will automatically lock.”

She took a breath and opened the lid, first spotting a gun and a stack of one-hundred-dollar bills. There was a black, oblong box, and she took it out and looked inside. It was filled with jewelry, her mother’s wedding ring catching her eye. These were all her mother’s pieces. Heirlooms by the look of them. Under the box were folded papers. She took them out and unfolded them. One was his will that left her everything, another was an insurance policy with her as the beneficiary. There was a flash drive also there. What was on it? She needed to know. Charlie quickly tucked it in her purse and then took the pictures of everything inside, returned the box to its slot and closed the door.

She walked back to the lobby to find Bryan and they left right as a police cruiser pulled up in front of the bank. Maybe they just learned of Moorhouse and her father’s trip. They needed to get the hell out of there before they recognized her.

She jumped into the passenger side and held her breath while Bryan started the car and pulled away.

“Anything important inside the box?”

“I did take pictures. There was a gun and a large stack of one-hundred-dollar bills. His will and insurance info was there along with a flash drive that is now in my purse.”

“We are going to need to see what’s on that before the police show up at your father’s door. Clearly, they now know he was with Moorhouse and will be looking for your dad."

"Should I tell the police he's missing—that we found the back door unlocked and his phone on the kitchen counter when we arrived?"

"Let me call Vince and see what he says, and we'll go from there."

He punched call on a number and waited. Vince answered on the third ring. "We have a problem. They know that Dennis was with Moorhouse before his murder. They were headed into the bank as we were leaving. I'm sure they will show up here soon. Should we reveal that Dennis is missing and that there was visible evidence he might have been abducted when we came to talk to him?"

"I don't see any way around it at this point. No one has heard from him. Did you find out anything in the bank?"

"I'll shoot you the pictures that Charlie took of his safety deposit box. That is what he accessed when he went in. Charlie also found a flash drive. We are headed back to Dennis's to see what's on it."

"All right. Keep me posted."

"Will do." Bryan ended the call.

He glanced at Charlie. "We better hope something on that drive can lead us to Dennis otherwise I'm afraid we might end up with a bad outcome."

This was Charlie's nightmare come true, and it was hard to not think the worst, but she was going to try to stay positive for her father's sake.

Chapter 16

Bryan sat at Dennis's desk and inserted the drive into its port. There were a handful of files, one drawing his attention. Why did Dennis have a file on Nathan Beal?

He opened the file and found a whole dossier on the man, to including allegations of sex trafficking. *Jesus Christ.*

"Am I reading that right?" Charlie leaned over his shoulder to look at the file. Her nearness set his entire body on fire, her breath so near his ear that it tickled all the way down his backbone. This woman was off limits and the only one to do this to him. *Dammit.*

Bryan cleared his throat and answered. "I think Nathan was into some nasty shit."

"Do you think my father was going to expose him? Could both our kidnappings have something to do with this file?"

"That's the question we need to find out."

"How do we do that?"

"He's in town and at the Pembroke Inn. I wanted to speak with him a few days ago, but there was no way to get past security there. But maybe you could. He does like you, right?"

She sighed. "Yes, but was it real? Maybe he was trying to control my father through me the whole time."

Bryan thought Charlie had a point. Was writing all

those letters a way to manipulate Charlie, hoping it'd work to get Dennis on a short leash? They needed to learn that. Did this mean Nathan had Dennis somewhere to keep him from exposing his crimes? They had to find out and fast because Dennis was a liability at this point. Why keep him alive?

"We need to hurry, Charlie. I think Nathan hired the men who kidnapped you and I think he did the same with your father. And frankly, your dad is better off dead to him at this point. We need to get in and see what Nathan has planned."

"Can't we get the police involved?"

"Not if that would trigger the immediate death of your father. We need to be covert about this to bring him home safely."

"Do you want me to call him and ask to meet?"

"Yes. Preferably out of that inn. Security there is impossible to breach, even for us."

As she reached for her father's phone, Bryan heard the front door slam. Both walked toward the door, thinking it was either Roy or Dennis. The latter would make life so much easier.

Bryan was the first to see Roy, who looked like he wanted to blow a gasket. "Is there a problem?"

"I guess you haven't seen the news this morning?"

Bryan glanced at Charlie, who frowned. "No, what happened?"

"That picture was released. I need to get back to Washington and try to mitigate the damage this could do to all Dennis's work on his committees."

"Make sure they know it was a doctored photo and that someone is trying to ruin my father's career."

"I'm going to grab my bag and go. I'm on a flight in

forty-five minutes. Call me when and if you find Dennis."

He left, and Bryan took a deep breath. "I think we knew this was a possibility."

"Yeah, but it was almost too fast. Someone wants my dad's influence diminished for some reason. We need to find out why after we find him."

Bryan nodded. "And I still think Nathan will lead us to that. Do you think you can go talk to him? Maybe see if he slips up and reveals something useful?"

"Yes. If he is involved in my father's disappearance, I'll do whatever is necessary to find him. Even using his interest in me to do so."

****

Charlie's nerves were frayed. She wasn't even sure she could get in to see Nathan. She'd tried to call the number her father had in his phone for him, but she got no answer. Maybe it was no longer in service, or perhaps he was busy holding her father somewhere. Just the thought caused steam to discharge from her body. If he was responsible for this whole mess, she planned to find out and get even one way or another.

"So, if they let you into the Inn, try not to be alone with Nathan. If possible, meet in the bar. I don't want him to grab you too, if he is indeed the kingpin in this kidnapping plot."

Charlie sighed, then got out of Bryan's SUV and walked up to the entrance to Pembrook. She immediately was met by security. "I need to speak to Nathan Beal, who is staying here. I'm Charlene Reed. He'll know who I am."

"Please stay here while I contact the front desk." The tall, muscular man dressed in black stepped inside and then returned a few minutes later. "Mr. Beal said he'd meet you in the Oak room. I'll show you the way."

She followed the guard through a set of security doors and down a long, gleaming hallway to an open arch that led to a restaurant that was stunning, with glass and chrome fixtures, clearly an exclusive, five-star establishment.

Charlie walked to the bar and took a seat at the end. Nathan would have no problem finding her here. To say she was nervous would be an understatement. She'd dealt with disgruntled husbands whose wives had just left them and had fewer jitters in their confrontations. Somehow, she had to appear unscathed, or he'd get suspicious.

The heavyset man in a red vest stepped over to her. "What can I get you?"

"A glass of your house white, please."

He nodded and walked over to get her order, then returned and placed it in front of her.

She quickly paid him, and he left.

With shaky hands, she lifted the glass and took a gulp of the wine, swallowing it for courage. Time seemed to stand still as she waited.

When he stepped through the entrance, Charlie could tell there was something different in his demeanor. This man seemed frightened, so unlike the guy who ran her father's campaign. Something had changed. Had her father threatened to expose him and had forced Nathan to go to extreme measures to protect himself? Was this why he looked scared now? Maybe he'd somehow gotten himself into a mess he couldn't get out of, or he was just playing a game with her. She had to be careful, or he might make her feel sorry for him, and that couldn't happen if he had her father stashed somewhere, planning to kill him.

He saw her and came toward her, causing her heart rate to accelerate. *Count to ten and breathe.*

"I was so surprised when they told me you were here," he said once he'd reached her.

Yeah, I just bet you were. "I needed to speak with you."

He frowned. "About?"

Boy, was he a great actor. Why hadn't she noticed this before?

"Have you spoken to my father since you've been in town?"

"I haven't. I did see those pictures that were released today. I imagine Dennis is not happy about them."

"They are fake. We know that much. Roy is working on getting the word out on that as we speak."

"That's good to know."

Why did his words not ring true to her? His jaw had tightened as if he were angry by the knowledge. Too bad. This man was clearly not her father's friend. Then again, if he was helping to traffic women for sex, he deserved to be in prison, not in politics.

"So, what did you need to talk to me about?" His question drew her back to her mission. Find her father.

"My father is missing. Is there anyone you can contact to help find him?" The ball was in his court. What would he suggest?

"Missing, you say? Since when?" Charlie studied his face. His expression said he didn't know this. Was he that good at hiding his feelings, or did he not know? This was something they were going to have to find out if they wanted to locate her father before something awful happened.

"Some time yesterday, I believe. The patio door was unlocked, and his phone was sitting on the kitchen table. He would never leave his phone if he could help it."

"Have you contacted the police?" Here was the question that he most wanted answers to. She could see it in his eyes. Getting police involved was key to catching him, and he didn't want that.

"Not yet," she said, "but we will if we don't find him soon."

"Let's keep the police out of it for now. I'll make some calls. See what I can find out about where he is. I'll call you when and if I learn anything. Him missing could all be his way of hiding from the media storm because of these pictures. Perhaps he knew they were going to be released, and that's why he's nowhere to be found."

"But then why leave his phone and the door unlocked?"

"They can track your phone, and maybe in his rush, he didn't lock the door. It could be that simple, Charlie. Go home and wait for my call." She doubted that, but she would leave. He wasn't going to tell her anything that would help. Not when he was protecting his own ass.

She rose and left the bar. In her heart, she knew her father was still alive—how long that would last was the million-dollar question.

Chapter 17

Bryan led Charlie up the stairs and bid her a good night. She had relayed everything that Nate had said, disappointing in its simplicity. Sterling was now doing a deep dive on the man to see if he owned anything in the area where he could stash Dennis, along with anything else they could find on his activities. In the morning, Bryan planned to follow the man's every move, having placed a tracker behind the wheel well of his rental car. Hopefully, Nathan Beal could lead them to Dennis, alive and well.

He walked to the spare room and stepped inside. The room was almost as big as his whole apartment on Albion. But that was okay with him. Byran didn't need much after all that time in the military and living in close quarters. Material things didn't fit into his equation. All he needed was a roof over his head and food to eat. That's why even with his physical attraction to Charlie, their worlds were too different to connect. She lived with all the amenities, things that were inconsequential to him. She was out of his league, and he knew it. Best to nip his sexual awareness of her in the bud right now, since nothing could come of it.

He sighed and walked to the adjoining bathroom. He slept so much better when he took a soothing shower before going to bed.

It took him twenty minutes, the one and only thing

that had changed since he left the corps. Military gave you five minutes to shower and dress before starting his morning. Twenty minutes gave him time to wind down, with the spray coursing over him after his long day. Something he needed with his ADHD. He had to slow down his brain so he could sleep.

Bryan stepped out of the shower and quickly dried, then brushed his teeth. He wrapped the towel around his waist and entered the bedroom, his phone on the bed chirping that he'd gotten a message.

If he read it, then his mind would again start spinning. Then again, it could be too important to wait until morning.

He grabbed his phone and saw it was from Vince. Yep. He was going to have to look at it.

—Dennis is okay. He's in hiding. He wanted Charlie to know so she wouldn't worry.—

But what about the dried blood they had found?

Are you sure it was from Dennis? Was it a phone call or message? Could they be trying to get Charlie to stop looking for him?—

—It was a text from a strange number. We might need to question it.—

Damned right. This was very likely a trick of Nathan's. The plan to tail him was still in place, and Bryan was going to follow it to the letter.

—I'll let you know what happens tomorrow. Good night.—

—You do that, and good night to you too.—

Now, Bryan was going to have trouble sleeping. Maybe he could slip down to the kitchen and see if they didn't have a soothing, herbal tea to help calm his mind.

He pulled on a pair of pajama bottoms and tied them.

In his bare feet, he padded out to the hall and down the flight of stairs, headed for the kitchen.

When he got close to the entrance, he heard a noise that put him on alert. He moved slowly, shocked to find Charlie in a pair of white and blue striped short pajamas and a light blue tee reaching up in a shelf for a box. "You couldn't sleep?" he asked, walking farther into the kitchen.

She turned, and her eyes widened. That was when he realized he'd forgotten to put on a shirt.

"I ah, I…"

"You what, Charlie?" he said, drawn to her legs that seemed to go on forever. He also noticed she wasn't wearing a bra, and her nipples were visible through the form-fitting tee. She wasn't overly large in the breast area, just enough for a hand to fill, a thought that caused an appendage to start to grow stiff. Dammit all to hell. So much for his thoughts from earlier taking hold. No amount of cajoling was going to keep his body from responding to the sight before him, and she was going to notice if he didn't leave or at least sit down.

He chose the latter.

"Did you need something?" she asked, refusing to look at him now.

"I was hoping you had an herbal tea to help me sleep."

She again turned to the cabinet, this time reaching up on her tiptoes to get that box she'd been trying to get earlier. This time, she got ahold of it, to his dismay, since it gave him full view of the cheeks of her firm ass. *Jesus, mother Mary.* He squeezed his eyes closed, thinking of something cold to extinguish the fire she'd just ignited inside his belly and below. His fingers were tingling to touch her, but he needed to remember she was a client and that nothing could happen between them.

She showed him the box of tea, a lavender/chamomile blend. "I guess you can't sleep either."

"I'm so worried about my dad."

Should he tell her about those texts? When he wasn't even sure they were from Dennis? Best not to get her hopes up just in case.

She walked over to the stove and put on the kettle, and then grabbed two mugs, placing a teabag in both. Charlie tried to look any place but at him, sure it was because he was shirtless.

Did it distract her? Made her body respond like his had to her appearance?

Time seemed to stand still, a clock ticking the only noise until the tea kettle whistled.

Charlie poured the steaming water into the mugs and then placed it back on the stove. She then brought the cups to the table, setting hers down and handing him the other, her eyes averting to his. Desire shone in them, only making it harder for him to not want to jump up and take her in his arms and show her how much she appealed to him.

Stop it, Bryan. Vince would be so disappointed in you right now. This was the first mission on your own, and you're contemplating sleeping with the client's daughter. You should be ashamed of yourself.

He cleared his throat and took a sip of his tea. *Just drink it and then go to bed.*

"Tell me a little bit about your job?" he suggested, thinking changing the subject might help keep his mind focused on something other than her body and wanting to explore every inch of it.

"What's to say? I deal with battered women. I've seen the worst situations. Even where the children are abused."

"You must think awful things about my gender."

"I'm thankful I've also seen good men to counter these awful individuals. I really believe that it is all in how a man is brought up—what they've encountered in their own lives. Yes, there can be exceptions to that, but for the most part, it is nurtured into them growing up."

Bryan had seen his share of this in the military. Divorce after divorce for his fellow soldiers who came back from combat with an anger inside them that they took out on the people closest to them. That was the reason why he remained single. He never wanted to put any woman through that with him. But it had also made life lonely and a bit sad, and then his own upbringing came back to reiterate that it was best not to get involved with anyone seriously. Sad and lonely, he could live with, hurting someone he loved, not so much.

****

Charlie found herself drawn to Bryan, so much so that she would have thrown herself at him had he not got up and left her sitting at the table once he'd finished his tea. There was something that held him back, something that had a wall built that was hard to get over. It was best to not try, but for some reason, Charlie wanted to anyway.

Bryan was one of those good men. She knew that within a day of meeting him. After all, he had saved her life. What more could she ask of him?

She downed the rest of her tea and placed both cups in the sink. She was going to go to bed. Tomorrow, hopefully, they'd find her father and then all would go back to normal. Then again, would they with those pictures circulating? Probably not, but they would cross that bridge when they had to.

Charlie left the kitchen and made her way to the staircase when Bryan was coming back down, the look on his face not at all good.

"What's wrong?"

"Vincent just called me. Someone broke into the office and ransacked everything. The only thing untouched was the safe room because they didn't know it was there."

"Do you know who is was?"

He shook his head. "Somehow, they wiped the surveillance cameras. This must be about your father. We've never had this happen before."

Charlie shook her head. What the hell was going on? What had her father got himself into for this to occur?

"Who would know how to do this and not be seen?"

"That's a very good question—one we need to find out as soon as possible. Vince has got Sterling looking for any surveillance on the street next to the building. Maybe they will find something there. Tomorrow, we need to follow Nathan and see where that leads us. You'd better get some sleep. After the break-in, it might be wise for me to keep my eyes open—just in case anyone is lurking around."

"Are you sure?"

"Yes. Go get some sleep. If anything else happens, I'll wake you."

"Okay. Night." Charlie took the stairs to her room, not sure if she could even rest. This whole thing was getting stranger by the day. But was Nathan Beal at the heart of it all? Was this about sex trafficking, or was there more to it than that? That was the question that needed answered, but the only two that could do that were the man himself and her father, and her dad was nowhere to be found.

Chapter 18

Bryan watched the sun come up, working on his fourth cup of coffee. Nothing had happened. No one prowling around. So, who had broken into Valor, and what were they looking for?

He had a thought. Could someone have gotten into Charlie's condo and searched there as well? They were going to have to check that. This was turning out to be bigger than just Nathan protecting himself—more people had to be involved—a sorted bunch that dealt in the underbelly of crime. It took some knowledge to hack into a camera feed and wipe it clean. It wasn't some two-bit thug that you could get off the street. This took skill, and Bryan wanted to know who the ringleader was in it all. In his gut, he didn't think it was Beal. That man was a political junkie—not someone capable of something like this.

"Is there more coffee?" Charlie's question startled him out of his thoughts.

"Yep. How'd you sleep?"

"How do you think? Is Beal still at the Pembrook?"

"His car is."

"Why don't you go shower, and we'll get ready to go," she said. "I've already done so."

Bryan jumped up. "Give me fifteen and we'll be on our way."

He took the steps two at a time.

In the guest room, he grabbed a change of clothes and went to turn on the shower. It took him a few minutes longer than fifteen, but he returned to the kitchen to find Charlie sipping her coffee, looking too pretty for her own good. This operation would be a whole lot easier if he wasn't so attracted to her.

"Ready?" He walked over to turn off the coffeepot.

She rose and put on an oversized sweater. "Where are we going first?"

"We need to find out if they were at your condo. I can't imagine they wouldn't check out your place before breaking into Valor."

Her eyes widened. "Why would they think I'd have anything of value to them? I had no knowledge of what my father was doing. Zero. Surely, they knew that after kidnapping me."

"I think this goes deeper than we both know. I wish Dennis would have been upfront with Vince about who he thought could have been at the heart of your abduction. Maybe then we'd have some idea how deep into the shit we were about to go."

She shrugged her shoulders. "Perhaps he didn't even know."

Somehow, Bryan was sure Dennis had known more than he'd been willing to reveal. Charlie was naive to think otherwise. But he'd keep that to himself for now. She was going to learn soon enough that her dad had gotten her into this mess, and it was still ongoing.

He allowed her out the door and made sure the door was locked before heading for his SUV.

Inside the cab, he cranked the engine over and plugged his phone into the GPS to show Nathan's location. He was going to make sure if the man left

Pembrook, he'd be right behind to find him where he landed.

He headed for Charlie's place, keeping an eye on Nathan's position. At the condo, he removed his phone, and they walked through her door. Inside, nothing looked out of the ordinary. So, it looked as if no one had been there.

Charlie looked relieved. "Apparently, they didn't get access to my place. What now?"

"Now, we grab some breakfast and stake out the Pembrook. If Nathan leaves, we'll follow him. I'm hoping he will lead us to your father." Bryan still wasn't going to reveal what Vince had told him. There was something fishy, and he didn't want her to get her hopes up. Not yet, at least.

On the road again, Bryan focused on driving while thinking about where to pick up something to eat. He'd had enough coffee for his eyes to be floating. Now, he needed to get something into his stomach. He was sure Charlie did as well. "Any preference about takeout?"

"Nothing too greasy."

"Okay. I got a place that makes a great breakfast sandwich that fits that bill."

Half an hour later, the two sat outside the Pembrook, eating their meal, parked where they could see Nathan's car and the front door, but he couldn't see them.

Bryan's phone rang and he saw that it was Sterling. Hopefully, he had that info on Beal.

"What you got?" he asked.

"I found something strange on Nathan's brother, Adam. He works for a container company. They supply shipping containers for cargo ships that travel all over the world."

A light went off in Bryan's brain. Containers that could carry trafficked people for the sex trade. This shit was getting dark and sinister.

"Where is the company located?"

"He's based in Norfolk."

"I think we need to delve deeper there. See what you can find on the company and Adam."

"I'll get right on it."

Bryan ended the call and glanced over at Charlie, who was licking something from her bottom lip. His eyes were glued. *Jesus Christ, get your mind on something important. Not how soft her lips look—how they'd feel next to his.*

"Apparently, Nathan's brother works for a company that makes large shipping containers that carry cargo worldwide. This might be Nathan's access to how he traffics these people. Sterling is looking deeper into this brother. We'll see what he finds."

Charlie shook her head. "Is this how he gets these women from all over the world? Does he stick them in these containers to survive from one point to the next? If so, Nathan is an animal who needs to be put down."

"I agree. But we have to prove this is what's happening first."

"There he is." Charlie pointed to the door where Nathan walked out, headed for his car.

Bryan started his vehicle. Now, they had to follow him and see where he led them.

****

Charlie was sickened at the idea of what Nathan Beal could be doing with his brother's help. Who in their right mind would think trafficking women for sex was an acceptable thing to do? How much money was involved, and was that all it was to him—a means to a flow of cash? Disgusting and perverted. Did he not think of women as equal to him? Was he one of those men who thought they were nothing but a vessel for pleasure?

How had her father not known about this sooner? Before the man worked to get him elected. Wouldn't that make him guilty by association? Some people would think so. Especially the media. Charlie didn't see how he'd come out of this unscathed.

She sat back in her seat, her whole perspective having changed. Here she was, working to protect women from awful men, and her father had hired one who was the epitome of horrible to them. Would she ever be able to trust her father's judgement again? She wasn't sure. But they needed to find him first. What if Nathan didn't lead them to him? How were they going to find him?

Bryan followed Beal's car out of the parking area, staying at least three car lengths away. He wouldn't lead them anywhere if he knew he was being trailed.

The man made a left turn. They mirrored the move. "Where do you think he'd headed? Doesn't this road lead to the warehouse district?"

"I believe so. That would be the perfect place to hide your father. In some warehouse."

The businesses started to become more sparse and large, metal structures were ahead on both sides of the street. Charlie had never been to this area before. It seemed dirty and sparse of activity. Ahead, Beal's taillights came on and he took a right. Bryan slowed his SUV to a crawl, taking the turn onto a road that had even fewer buildings, one on the end. That seemed to be where Nathan was headed.

Bryan pulled over, took out his phone and punched a number. "Sterling, I need some info on a warehouse on Industrial Ave. Looks like the last on the street.

"Hang on. I'll see what I can find."

As they waited, Charlie's heart started to pound in her chest. This might be where her father was. They were this close to getting to him. She could hardly contain herself. Charlie wanted to charge ahead and find him, but they needed to wait to see what they could possibly run into going inside. One thing was for sure: when she did see her father, the two were going to have a long talk about the company he kept—inside and outside of the bedroom.

"Bryan. It's titled to some holding company. So, there is no way of knowing who owns the building."

"Shit." Bryan glanced at the structure and then back to Charlie. "Okay, thanks. Anything else on Beal?"

"Not yet. I'll call if I find anything of importance."

He ended the call and blew out a long breath. "I'm going to try to sneak in and see if I can't find your father. You stay here."

Charlie shook her head. "I'm going with you."

"Look, Charlie. I don't want to have to worry about you getting hurt."

"Then don't. I'm going, and you aren't stopping me. So, let's go."

He looked like he wanted to object, but instead, opened his car door and got out. Charlie did the same, and they headed for the door where Beal entered.

"Once we get inside, follow close behind me. Don't make any sound."

She nodded, then, with her heart pumping hard in her chest, they stepped inside the building, a humming noise instantly drawing her attention. What was it? It seemed to be in another area of the building. He started to move, and she inched her way behind him, not wanting to anger him for not following orders. She'd learned early to listen when told something by her father. She would do the same with Bryan. He didn't have to let her go. He could have insisted she stay in the car. She appreciated that he'd allowed her to go.

The two shadowed the wall, Bryan stopping short when angry voices echoed around them. Charlie tried to make out what was being said, but it was garbled.

Gunfire erupted, and Bryan turned them both around and they left the same way they came.

Outside again, Bryan grabbed her hand and dragged her back to the car. "We have to go back, Bryan. My father could be in there."

"I'm going back. You are staying in the car. Understand?" His words were said with such force that Charlie knew he meant it. She was going to listen. She nodded as he reached into the glove box and retrieved his weapon. "Lock the doors and keep your head low. If I don't come out in fifteen minutes, get the hell out of here and call the police."

"Okay." Charlie got into the SUV and locked the doors. She wasn't going to defy him this time. He was putting his life on the line going back inside. She wasn't going add to the danger by not doing exactly what he told her to do.

Chapter 19

Bryan opened the metal door, his eyes quickly readjusting to the fluorescent lighting twenty feet above.

He had no idea what he was about to stumble into. Only that whoever was there had guns blazing. Hopefully, if Dennis was here, he was still alive. Shots were fired, but he had no idea if they'd hit their target.

He moved slowly, headed in the direction where he'd heard the gunfire. Again, angry voices stopped him in his tracks. Clearly, the shots had been to get someone's attention, not kill them.

He inched his way toward the voices, not wanting them to hear him coming. He needed the element of surprise since there were a least two of them.

Ahead, a bright light coming from a door had him heading toward the entrance. They were inside. He slid along the wall, stopped just short of the entry. Bryan was close enough now to hear what was being said.

"Goddammit. Why can't you do one thing right?"

"You never told us we'd have some type of special forces coming to save her."

"That's because I didn't know. What about Dennis? Where the fuck is he?"

Bryan released a breath. So, Nate didn't have him. That was good. But then, where was Charlie's father and what was he doing?

He could leave right now, but maybe he could learn

more from this conversation.

"The man wasn't home when we got there, though. It looked like trouble when the back door was open, and his phone sat on the table. Is there someone else who could have taken him?"

"Not that I know of. Dennis is smart. Maybe he staged the place to look like he was abducted. Right now, I need you idiots to find out where Charlie is staying."

"Why? Do you want us to grab her again?"

"Hardly. I could have done that last night if I wanted to. I just want to keep track of her. Dennis loves his daughter. He will try to get to her. If we know where she is, we will find Dennis eventually."

"Well, she isn't at Valor. We know that."

"Do we? They may have hidden her there somewhere. Just find her if we want to get paid and do it before the shit hits the fan."

Bryan chose that moment to leave. Their conversation was over. Now he needed to get Charlie back to the safe house. Charlie's security was paramount, and now they knew this was all about her father and finding him. If she was in a secure place, Dennis would come to her when he felt it was safe to do so. Bryan was sure they wouldn't come back to Valor. It'd be too risky, which meant that was the safest place for her now.

He was going to run back to her father's, pack their stuff and get back into the safe room until Dennis showed up to join them. Then maybe they'd learn what this whole mess was all about.

He retraced his steps out to his SUV, jumped in and started the engine. "Your father isn't here. Nathan doesn't have him. We need to get back to his place, pack our bags and go to the safe house. I heard Nathan wants to get to your father through you. We can't let that happen. They'd never try to break into Valor again. It would be too risky. And they can't access the safe room. I doubt they even know it's there. Hopefully, your father will come to us when he's ready."

"You are sure Nathan doesn't have him?"

"Yes. Beal has no idea where he is. For now, we need to help keep it that way." Bryan turned around and headed south. It would take them a few minutes to gather their things, and then another twenty to get to Valor. Once they were there, he'd think of a plan as to what to do next. Clearly, that phone call Vince had gotten was for real. That meant if Dennis contacted him again, he'd know that Charlie was safe in the panic room and that it would be wise for him to join them until whatever mess he'd gotten himself into was resolved and Nathan and his henchmen were arrested for kidnapping.

****

The last place Charlie wanted to be was sidelined in the panic room again, nowhere to go, not even a window to look out to see the world turning around her. But if it kept her father from being abducted, then she'd do it for him.

She stepped out of the room she'd been given last time and glanced around. Bryan must be in the other room, hopefully getting some rest. She had yet to see the man sleep. How he functioned was beyond her.

Her stomach started to grumble, and she walked over to the small kitchen to see what was in the refrigerator.

Anything you'd possibly need was inside. She pulled out everything to make a sandwich, and then found a plate and a glass for wine she also grabbed.

Maybe a little alcohol would make her less edgy.

As she was sitting down to eat, the door into the panic room opened, and Vince walked in, smiling at her. "Where's Bryan?"

"I think he's sleeping. I swear that man can survive on as little as possible."

"Yeah, the military can do that to you."

"Anything on my father?

He shook his head. "Nope. But don't think the worst. My gut says Dennis is in a safe place and will contact us when he can. Try not to worry. I'm going to let Bryan sleep. Tell him to call me when he can. Enjoy your wine and sandwich."

Charlie smiled and watched him leave, sighed, then took a long swallow of the red wine. What could it hurt? She might finish the bottle off and then try and get some sleep as well.

"Did I hear Vince?" Bryan's question made her heart stop. The man was too stealthy for his own good.

"He just left. He told me to have you call when you can."

He came to sit beside her on the island chair. "Did he say what he needed to talk to me about?"

She shook her head. "I think he didn't want to say anything to me. You military types are so close-mouthed about everything. You are just lucky I'm used to that, or I might be offended."

He gave her a hearty laugh that drew her attention to his mouth. Damned if he didn't have the most appealing lips she'd ever seen on a man.

She swallowed hard and returned her attention to her sandwich. "I hope you don't mind me making myself at home."

"Not at all, Charlie. This might be your home away from home for the next few days. You might as well break it in now."

She pointed to the fixings on the island top. "Would you like me to make a sandwich too?"

"Let me call Vince first, and then I'll join you." He rose and walked away, taking his phone out of the back pocket of his jeans, an action that had Charlie staring at his nicely shaped ass. *I don't do military men. I don't do military men*, repeated like a mantra in her mind.

Why did Bryan make her forget that? There was something about him, not just a physical thing, but something more. She wished she could put a finger on what it was so she could vanquish it for good. The last thing she needed to worry about was controlling her libido when her father was missing.

Bryan returned, his expression instantly concerning her.

"What's wrong?"

"Nothing."

He was lying, but why?

"Please tell me what's happening. I have a right to know."

"Actually, you are better off not knowing, Charlie. Trust me on this."

"Is my father all right?"

"As far as I know, yes."

Charlie couldn't let it go. She needed answers. "So, it's not about him?"

"No, but he could have known this was coming since he's the head of the judicial committee and may be the reason Nathan kidnapped you."

Chapter 20

Bryan had already shared more than he wanted to with Charlie. She had enough to worry about. It was best to leave her in the dark for now. There wasn't anything they could do about what was about to happen anyway.

"Why don't we eat and then try to get some sleep. If I thought you needed to know, I would tell you, Charlie. Right now, we have to sit still and wait to hear from your father."

She stared at him for the longest time, to the point his skin started to prickle. She certainly had a way of making his body react one way or another. It was like a superpower; one he didn't appreciate.

"Eat." He pointed to her sandwich while picking up his own. Best to act normal. Tomorrow was going to be a long day, and he needed to be at his best if the shit hit the fan.

"Do you have a girlfriend, Bryan?"

Where the hell did that come from? She sure changed subjects fast. "No, I don't. I haven't had time for any kind of social life. Why Sanderson? I know it's just an arrangement but why him? The guy is a womanizer. Why would you want your name to be connected to his in any way?" She could have chosen just about anyone who would be a better fit for a pretend boyfriend.

"He's nicer than he seems." She took another bite of

her sandwich.

"I talked to him over the phone. He was a jerk. And frankly, didn't seem at all worried when you were missing."

"He was always nice to me."

"Maybe because of your father's power and influence?"

"Perhaps. I don't know. Why does it matter now?"

"I guess it doesn't." He'd meant to distract her from Vince's call, but it had only dredged up more questions. Why would a man of his means want Charlie to pretend to be his girlfriend? Was it what it seemed, or was there more to it? After they went to bed, he'd contact Sterling and get him to do another deep dive into him. Maybe he'd been part of this abduction plan as well as Beal. This could be much bigger than any of them even thought. Corruption seemed to be around every corner since the new administration took over. Another reason he had decided to leave the service. He didn't want to be at the whims of a lunatic, warmonger.

What was going to be revealed tomorrow? All he knew was that something was coming out from a closed-door session, and it was supposed to be shocking. Was it about Dennis, or was it something Dennis knew was coming and Beal wanted him to stop? He'd learn soon enough. But right now, he needed to keep Charlie out of it—distract her until they went to bed. Just the thought had him imagining her in his. *Dammit all to hell.* What was it about this woman who had his thoughts going to the worst place. Dennis and Vince would murder him if he touched her. That's why he had to keep his mind and hands off her.

He took the last bite of his sandwich and went to the

sink to rinse the plate, and then placed it into the dishwasher.

As soon as she finished hers, he was going to usher her to her room. Best to not be around her when his body seemed to be revolting against his common sense. Not something he'd had to worry about until he met her.

She came over to rinse her plate and tucked it into the tray of the dishwasher. "Want to watch some TV?"

Her nearness was too much for Bryan. Charlie was the only woman he'd ever had this attraction to, to the point that his brain went haywire.

Instead of walking away, she turned toward him, her breath just inches from his neck, stirring up goose bumps. *Dammit all to hell.*

She continued to look at him with those eyes that reached into his soul. Without thinking, he leaned in and kissed her lightly on her lips, the petal soft contact ending any common sense he had as he folded her into his arms and deepened his kiss, plying his tongue against her mouth and she opened for him to taste her sweetness. His hands moved down to cup her ass, so firm and round—so incredibly perfect.

Instinctively, he bucked against her, having gone too long without intimacy.

A noise across the room had him flying back, his attention on the man now standing in the doorway. *Dennis. Shit. Shit. Shit.*

"Daddy!" Charlie raced to get to him.

Bryan was relieved that the man was okay, but now knew he'd be in deep shit for kissing his daughter.

****

Charlie wrapped her arms around her father, more than relieved to see him. She held tight for longer than she ever had, afraid if she let go, he'd disappear. Finally, she pulled back and looked at him, his face looking like it had aged ten years since she'd seen him. "What is going on, Daddy? Where have you been? Why did it look as if someone had taken you at the house?"

He held up a hand, looking flustered and like he was about to collapse. "I need to sit down, Charlie. I've been on the move for days."

She followed him to the couch. He dropped down and leaned his head back. Was he going to make her wait to learn anything? He owed her since something he'd done had gotten her kidnapped and running for her life for the past three days.

"Can I get some water?" he said to Bryan, who still stood where she'd left him. He retrieved a bottle from the fridge and delivered it to her father.

He removed the cap and downed half of it. "Thanks for finding Charlie."

Bryan nodded. Was he worried about them being caught kissing? Charlie was still trying to catch her breath. The man could kiss like no other, had her thinking things she hadn't. Dangerous and not sustainable. She knew that. Military men were off limits. But was he still military? Why was she suddenly thinking he wasn't? Had that kiss changed everything? Had he had the same reaction, or was it just her?

She shooed the thought and returned her attention to the man sitting on the couch, still not willing to answer any of her questions.

"Where have you been hiding, Daddy?"

"In plain sight," he said, clearly evading the inquiry.

"That's not really telling me anything. Try again."

"It's best you don't know."

Charlie glared at him. Maybe if he'd have told her what was happening before, she might have not put herself at risk of being kidnapped. For him not to be honest now just made her angry with him. "I want to know why I was abducted."

He squeezed his eyes closed and took a long breath. "I'm afraid if I disclose what I know, it will only put you in more danger, Charlie. I never dreamed these people would try to get to me through you. I didn't even know how deep this rot went until two days ago. I was almost taken myself. I was able to slip out the back door, and I've been hiding ever since."

"Hiding from who? Nathan Beal? I know he has something to do with this." Bryan glanced at her, then her father.

"Yes. Nathan is only part of this cabal. I was asked to meet with someone six weeks ago, a man who said he had something that needed to be exposed in some members of Congress. I wasn't sure I should even meet with him. It sounded like some kind of conspiracy bullshit. I went out of curiosity. He had some very compelling evidence and wanted me to help expose this. I still wasn't on board, or sure it was true, until the man I met with ended up dead."

Charlie sucked in a labored breath. "That wasn't the man you went to the bank with, was it?"

"No. That was another unfortunate death. Probably by the same hand. The man I met with died under suspicious circumstances a month ago. It was a car crash that ended with him burning to death in his vehicle. It was just too convenient."

"Why were you with that man at that bank? I found the flash drive and read the file on Beal. Who else is involved?" Bryan asked.

"I don't think it's wise for me to say right now. It just puts the both of you at risk."

"We already are, Daddy. We have been running for days as well. I met with Nathan the other night, trying to find out if he knew where you were."

Her father shook his head. "Beal is dangerous. You need to stay away from him. You aren't allowed to go anywhere until this is over and certain people are eliminated."

Her eyes widened. "Eliminated how?"

"I don't know yet. Let's just say there are certain people in high places working on this as we speak. Tomorrow, something is going to come out about me. It was blackmail that Beal tried to shut me up with. Deepfake shit that will put into question my moral ethics. I may even be asked to resign. I'm going to refuse, of course, because what I will bring later will end at least ten congressmen's careers."

"I've seen the pictures, Daddy. Are there other people besides members of Congress involved?"

"Yes, but I'm not going to reveal them until I have to. They are very powerful people, and they are the ones who want me to be mute or dead, whatever comes first."

"Have you spoken to Vince?" Bryan asked.

"Not in the past twenty-four hours. Why?"

"Our tech guy looked at those pictures. We know they are pieced together. Can't you step up and tell everyone they were faked?"

"Who is going to believe me, especially when those compromised congressmen are using their voices against me?"

"What about that young woman carrying your child?

She is so young, Daddy."

"I don't know what this woman told you, but she's lying. If she's pregnant, it's not mine. I never slept with her. She is part of this whole plan to discredit me."

Charlie's mouth dropped open. She'd seemed so sincere. How many people were involved in this cover-up? "I seriously thought I was going to have a sibling. How could she lie like that?"

"Money. There is a lot on the line for the ones involved. This young lady is just a bit player. Willing to say anything to get paid.

"Now, I have to sleep. I'll take the couch. That way, I can keep an eye on the doors. Make sure they all stay closed."

Charlie's face heated. He was referring to the kiss and where that could have led. She took a quick glance at Bryan, who looked flushed as well. Meaning acknowledged and understood. No sleeping with the help. "Night, Daddy. Tomorrow you are going to tell me everything, I don't care who it endangers."

Chapter 21

Bryan didn't like how Dennis refused to delve into what all this mess was about. Why was he hiding it from them? Did Vince know what was going on? Did they think it was best to keep him and Charlie in the dark? Would they find out before the whole world knew? The mere idea of that pissed him off since he'd risked his life to save Dennis's daughter.

He shoved the covers aside, still about eight hours short of a good night's sleep.

He grabbed a change of clothes from his duffel, thinking later he was going to have to do a load of laundry. He was running out, though he was sure the safe room had spares.

He stepped into the bathroom to shower. What was going to be announced today? Was it what they thought? Dennis's fake pictures, or did they have a deep-fake video to go along with it? The things they could do to ruin a person's life without it being true were unbelievable.

When it does hit, their only hope was to prove it was faked. Then again, people seemed to believe what they wanted to, to hell with the truth. That's how they ended up with this administration. Too many didn't have critical thinking brains, and that hurt their country from the bottom up.

Bryan quickly washed, then stepped out and dried

himself. After dressing, he brushed his teeth, combed his hair and left the room. Dennis was in the kitchen, coffee cup in hand, leaning against the cabinet next to the stove. His attention was on Charlie's door. For such a stern, military man, you could tell how troubled he was by the deep V in his forehead. Yes, this man held deep secrets that were wearing on him physically.

"Morning." Bryan headed over to get a cup of coffee. As he was pouring, he asked Dennis, "Did you get any sleep?"

The man sighed. "A few hours. How about you?"

"About the same. I really wish you could tell me what is going on, Dennis."

"Like I told Charlie, you two are better off not knowing right now. Once it's out there for anyone to see, there is no way to not worry. Just try not to think about it right now."

That statement alone only caused more dread. This was majorly bad. He could see that now.

Bryan took a sip of coffee, all sorts of scenarios running through his head. Top of the list—a terrorist attack. But would Nathan Beal have anything to do with something that horrendous? He really couldn't see that in the man. Yet, he'd never imagine him kidnapping Charlie to keep Dennis quiet, either. If life and limb were on the line, maybe anyone could lower themselves to evil. Byran would hope he wouldn't, but then again, he didn't have someone he loved so much that his perspective could be skewered.

He clamped his hand tightly around his mug. "Can I ask if Vincent knows?"

"Yes," Dennis said without hesitation.

For Vince to know and keep it a secret meant it was

worse than bad. Was the end of the world coming? Should he prepare for that possibility? It's not like he'd run to his father to make things right. The man didn't deserve that.

A door opened, and he looked over to see Charlie stepping out of the other bedroom, looking stunningly beautiful in a cream-colored V-neck sweater and a pair of black, form-fitting jeans. Damned if just seeing her didn't cause his skin to warm, especially after their shared kisses last night. She had to have the softest lips he'd ever kissed. The one thing he'd like to do if the world was ending, was spend every minute with her in bed.

Bryan shook the thought, knowing her father would beat him senseless if he knew the direction of his wayward thoughts. *Remember where you are and who is here.*

Charlie reached them, her eyes looking as red as theirs. Clearly no one had gotten much sleep. Too many thoughts of what was about to happen. Except, Bryan knew more than Charlie did, and that wasn't a good thing.

"Coffee?" Bryan asked, her affirmative nod making him get her a cup.

She took the coffee and took a sip, her attention on her father. "Do you know when this briefing will occur today?"

"No. I imagine it'll be this afternoon some time."

"And you can't tell me anything more?"

"No. I'm going to go take a shower. I'll make breakfast when I come back."

He left, and Bryan drank more of his coffee. He wasn't going to wait for Dennis to make breakfast. He needed to stay busy after what he learned. Idle minds conjured up worst case scenarios. He'd go crazy doing that. Best to stay busy.

He walked over the refrigerator and pulled out some fruit that was in a clear container. He'd get Charlie to cut some up when he made a vegetable and cheese omelet.

He grabbed a knife and handed it to her. "Can you cut up some melon and strawberries while I make eggs?"

"Of course."

She went in search of a bowl, then sat down and started, keeping her head down while working. She was thinking about something. Bryan would love to know what.

Instead, he reached back into the fridge for the stuff he needed and got another knife to cut up the veggies.

At the stove, he placed a large cast-iron skillet on a burner, turned it on and drizzled some olive oil in the pan. He'd need to start the cooking process on top, then place it in the oven for twenty minutes.

Once it was inside and on three fifty, he turned back to Charlie who was nibbling on a ripe strawberry, his eyes instantly drawn to her mouth. If only she wasn't a client's daughter, and the shit wasn't about to hit the fan.

He blew out a breath and set the timer on the stove. *Keep your mind on safe things.*

"More coffee?" He needed another shot of caffeine since sleep had practically evaded him.

She slid her cup in front of her and nodded. "Yes, and keep it coming."

****

Charlie studied Bryan while he wasn't watching, totally smitten with the man. She'd always been level-headed when it came to the opposite sex, especially in her line of work, but he was different. That kiss had sealed it for her. He was the man she wanted, and hopefully, when they were out of this mess, the two could explore that.

He turned from taking the eggs from the oven, and she looked down at her coffee. No way did she want him to see her adoration, not until she knew he had feelings for her first.

He placed the skillet on a towel in the middle of the island and reached up for some plates.

As he was spooning out portions on the first, her dad returned, his hair still wet, wearing a tan T-shirt and a pair of fatigues.

He came and sat beside her, his hand squeezing her shoulder. “I think I forgot to ask how you were doing?”

She sighed deeply. This was the man she knew and loved. “I’m okay. I just wish I knew more about what was going on.”

“I know, and I hate keeping you in the dark, but right now it’s best for you overall.” He pointed to the pan. “This looks good.”

Bryan spooned some onto his plate and reached behind him to retrieve the coffeepot. “More coffee?”

“Just half a cup. When you get to be my age, you learn, less is more.”

Bryan leveled her cup after giving her father half. “Eat up.”

Charlie handed her father the bowl of fruit she’d cut up, and he spooned some onto his plate.

She took a bite of eggs, thinking that Bryan was not only great to look at but was an excellent cook as well. What else was he good at? The thought caused a rush of heat to race across her body. There was no mistaking her lust for him, and as long as they remained in close quarters, that was only going to grow.

The door to the panic room opened, and Vince watched in, spotted them and started their way.

"I guess I showed up just in time."

Bryan went to get another plate and a cup to fill with coffee. "Has anything happened yet?" Bryan asked once he was seated again.

Vincent shook his head. "I got a call from Dennis's chief of staff. The Justice committee insists on Dennis being in-house tomorrow morning. Said it was mandatory."

"Yeah, I'm not feeling good about that." Her father gave Vince a look of frustration.

"I agree. I assume it could be a trap of some kind. We put a surveillance team on that warehouse. Something there is important to this plan Beal has. If anything leaves, we will follow it to wherever it ends up."

"Are we talking terrorist plot?" Bryan asked.

Charlie's eyes widened at the thought. Was this what it was? She thought it was all about trafficking people. Was there a bigger plot afoot? The mere idea gave her a sick stomach, and she pushed her plate away.

"How can we just sit here when something catastrophic could be about to happen?"

"We are doing all we can for now, Charlie. Try not to think about it," her father suggested.

"Are we? Shouldn't we contact the police? The FBI would be more equipped to deal with this than us."

"Unfortunately," Vince said, cutting in. "We don't know if any of those agents there are involved."

"Oh my God." Dread took hold, causing her skin to

erupt into goose bumps. This was far worse than she thought and seemed to be getting more dangerous by the second. Maybe it was best she didn't know. Because knowing might make her lose her mind.

No. She had to stay calm. Whatever was about to happen was going to occur, and she needed to keep it together to help where she could. They needed everyone to be straight-up calm. She wasn't going to embarrass her father. He'd taught her to be strong, and that's exactly what she'd be.

"So, is there anything we can do now?"

"I'm glad you asked. I need you to contact your boyfriend. I'll write down everything I want you to say," Vincent said, shocking her. Why call him?

"I'm confused. Why would you want to get Sanderson involved?"

"It's merely a hunch, Charlene, but after getting our hands on Beal's phone records, it appears Mr. Emery is part of this plot."

Charlie's jaw dropped. This couldn't be true. What would Sanderson have to gain? "Why?"

"Where does Sanderson Emery get all his money? He has some pretty sketchy friends that Sterling found when he dug deeper into the man's past. His father was sent to prison for five years for money laundering. I don't think the apple falls that far from the tree here."

"Are you saying he used me to get to my father?"

"That I'm not sure of, but who knows."

"Daddy, if this is true, I'm so sorry. I had no idea. We met at a party and talked. If he planned that meeting, I feel stupid."

"How could you possibly know his intent?" Bryan started to reach for her hand, but picked up his cup instead. Would he have touched her if they were alone? She'd never know. But she appreciated him trying to make her feel better, even though she didn't. If her connection to Sanderson started this ball rolling, then she was going to have to be the one to bring it to a stop. How, was the question.

"What do you want me to tell Sanderson?" Charlie knew what she'd like to say, but that wasn't going to help.

"I want you to tell him the police called to tell you that your father was killed in a car accident. You've got to make him believe it. That way, when Dennis shows up in Washington, they won't be prepared. We are going to bring this whole cabal down, and we are going to do it without anyone firing a shot."

Chapter 22

Bryan couldn't believe that Dennis had insisted that Charlie go to Washington with him. Which meant he had to go as well to keep her safe. They also had five of the team to tail Dennis once he entered the capital building tomorrow morning. Until then, they'd lie low at a friend of Vincent's that was out of the country, a two-story Tudor-style house twenty miles east of the Capital.

With the main characters thinking Dennis was dead, they should all be safe, and once they reached their destination, they would formulate their plan. If they didn't do everything by the letter, something bad might happen, and Dennis could either end up dead, or his career would be.

"We are on approach," the pilot of the private plane said over the intercom.

Bryan fastened his seatbelt and laid his head back in the seat. Charlie sat across from him, her father next to her. She was happy that he was there. He could see the relief on her beautiful face. They were just days away from going their own way now, and he wasn't sure how he felt about that fact. She'd been his responsibility for four days, and he kind of liked having her around.

The plane descended and landed in record time. A large van was waiting for them on the tarmac.

They loaded all their stuff in the back and got inside, Charlie sitting next to him. Her nearness seemed to drain the air out of the cab. Once they reached the house, he was going to get a room and stay there. Tomorrow, he'd again have to stick to her like glue; now, he needed some distance.

The ride to the house took thirty minutes. The home was surrounded by concrete and steel gating. It was more like a compound than a family residence. Bryan wondered about the people who owned it. Why would they need this type of protection for themselves?

This time, they unloaded the van and walked to the front entrance, punching in a code on the door before stepping inside.

Bryan entered, trying hard not to gawk. He'd never been in such luxury before. What did a place like this cost, just outside the capital?

Too much for his measly budget. This was what Charlie deserved, and he'd never be able to give it to her. Just another reason to stay the course and avoid her for the rest of the day.

He hefted his duffel over his shoulders and went in search of one of the upstairs bedrooms. The first door he opened, the bedroom was huge. He didn't need anything so elaborate. It took him another three doors to find a small bedroom, one that would suit him fine.

He placed his bag on the dresser and kicked off his boots. What he needed more than anything was a few hours of sleep.

He sat on the mattress and sighed.

When he was about to doze off, a knock had him opening his eyes and looking around. The door opened, and Charlie stepped inside, closing them in together. Again, the air became stifling.

Why couldn't he get away from her? Didn't she

understand how hard it was to be around her without wanting to touch her, to kiss her?

"I need to talk to you."

He pulled himself up to a sitting position and patted the mattress beside him.

She sat down next to him, her hesitation to talk confusing him. "What's on your mind?" Bryan thought that inviting her to sit on the bed hadn't been such a smart move. It conjured up all kinds of inappropriate actions.

"How do they know Sanderson was involved in all of this? When I spoke to him, he sounded genuinely sorry for my loss. Could he be that good an actor?"

"The man is all about money and power, Charlie. If enough is at stake, anyone can lie."

"Even you?"

"I don't care about money or power. It was never a priority for me. What you see is what you get."

She sat quietly for some time, causing him to wonder what she was thinking.

"I haven't known you long, Bryan, but I trust you, and I like what I see."

He swallowed hard. Was she saying she thought he was handsome? Was she trying for a repeat of their kisses from yesterday? So much for getting away to think. She was here, making it impossible not to grant her that wish.

He clasped the back of her neck and drew her close. His lips grazed hers, the blood in his brain causing a rush. He nipped at her mouth, teasing, tantalizing her, and as his hands started to roam over her back, Dennis calling Charlie's name had him jumping up and walking away to look out the window.

He heard the door open and close, then she called to

her father. *Dammit, Charlie. You really messed with my libido, something I had been in full control over until I met her.*

Sleep would be impossible now. He might as well go find out if they'd come up with a plan for tomorrow. Bryan just hoped that whatever it was, no one was going to end up losing their life.

He found all the Bolton crew in the kitchen, the refrigerator door open, completely stocked with food.

"You want a beer?" Hank Brady asked, holding a bottle out to him. Bryan took it and twisted off the top, taking a long swallow. This is what he needed after that kiss. Being with the guys would keep him distracted and his mind off Charlie. He was pretty sure Dennis was making sure they were not in close quarters since he'd witnessed the kiss from last night. He clearly didn't think Bryan was good enough for her, and frankly, he'd be right. She deserved someone who could give her diamonds, fancy cars and huge houses. All he had was that ring he'd bought at the pawn shop. He couldn't give her anything worth what she deserved, and he needed to remember that.

****

Charlie still wondered what her father had wanted when he called her. Had he known she was with Bryan, worried that they were doing something he wouldn't approve of?

She followed her father down the hall and out a pair of French doors, the backyard filled with lush trees and flowering plants. There was a large pool lined with a deck and chaise lounge chairs. If she had brought a suit, she would have taken a swim. It had been a while since she'd done laps, something she did daily while in school.

Now, she didn't seem to have time for anything that she'd once enjoyed.

"Do you have a problem with Bryan?" she asked her father once they'd reached the poolside and sat in the chairs.

"What do you mean? I never said I didn't like him."

She stared at him. "But you don't want me left alone with him."

He cleared his throat, looking like he wanted to say something but wasn't sure if he should. "Just say it, Daddy. I know you want to."

"I remember when you told me you were never going to get involved with a military man? What changed?"

What had changed? It was Bryan. He was attractive and competent. He saved her life and hadn't given it a second thought. Who wouldn't want him? She was surprised he wasn't married with a handful of kids. To her, he was a catch. Why didn't her father see that?

"There is just something special about him. Bryan's what people would consider hero material. He came to my rescue and didn't waver in risking his own life for mine, not for a minute."

"I understand that you see him in that way, but do you think he can give you what I have? You like nice things, Charlie, and your non-profit doesn't even cover your condo, let alone the closet filled with designer clothing and accessories."

Charlie was taken aback by her father's words. Why hadn't he said anything before about her lifestyle? Now, she felt bad. Was he right, though? Could she live a minimalist's life? She didn't know where Bryan lived, but she was sure it was nothing like her place.

"I'm sorry, Daddy. I guess I just didn't see what all you paid for. I need to take a look at myself and maybe make some changes."

"That's not what I'm saying, sweetie. I'm just not sure Bryan is a good fit for you, that's all."

"But he's the first man I've ever liked this much. That's got to mean something. You were a military man, dating a rich girl. How did Momma's parents feel about her being with you? Were there concerns on their part?"

He blew out a breath. "Yes. Her father told her the same thing I'm telling you now. How did you get smarter than me?"

She reached over and squeezed his hand. "You are simply being a father. Just know that Bryan is worthy, Daddy. If we do start dating, then I don't want you to worry. I'm a big girl, and I am going to step up more. I want to be able to make you proud."

"You do make me proud, Charlie. Look at the work you do for women in trouble. It's a calling that can't be easy to deal with all the time. I don't know how you do it."

Voices from inside the house had them turning to see the Valor men stepping out of the house, all carrying a bottle of beer. Charlie's attention went straight to Bryan, who seemed to be avoiding looking at her. Was he having second thoughts about them starting something? Maybe he didn't want anything past a few stolen kisses. How would she handle that? Would she be able to go on knowing he lived in the same town and not see him after this mess was over, and his protection was no longer needed? Somehow, he knew she couldn't. She wanted to be with him and not in a friendly way like with Sanderson, not that she ever had one inkling of attraction to him. He was a means to an end. A good thing since he was using her to get to her father, but why? What did he have to do with Beal? Was he a part of this trafficking thing?

She was going to know soon enough. Right now, she planned to go find one of those beers and enjoy her night. Tomorrow could end in tragedy if things didn't go her way, and she didn't want to think about that now.

"I'm going to get one of those beers. Do you want one?"

"Sounds good. Grab some snacks as well."

Charlie rose and headed for the door. She may just have one too many drinks and forget about what's to come. In the morning, everything would be different, and she could go back to worrying again.

Chapter 23

Bryan woke with a start, gunfire erupting from somewhere in the house.

He shoved the covers aside and jumped into his jeans, reaching for the handgun he'd tucked into the side dresser drawer.

As quietly as he could, he eased his door open and listened, a single round going off again, clearly coming from the ground floor. He had two choices: go see who was firing the shots, or find Charlie and make sure she was safe.

He chose the first since he was sure Dennis would make sure his daughter was out of harm's way.

He slipped down the hall, then took the steps down to the ground floor, looking left, then right when he hit the landing. Who was firing those shots?

As Bryan made his way through an archway that led to the back, where they had spent the evening lounging by the pool. He saw that the doors were wide open. He knew that they had locked them when they'd come inside.

Someone had gotten in and was shooting at a target, but who?

He listened intently, hearing a moaning sound coming from the breezeway. He ducked down and crawled to a form he saw lying next to a small table. When he reached them, he saw it was Kurt, one of their men. He was holding his shoulder where blood was covering his light colored shirt. Thank God the wound didn't appear to be life-threatening. "Where's the shooter?" he asked him, his eyes darting around to see any movement.

"I think he headed down to the lower bedrooms. Probably after Dennis."

Bryan nodded, then started toward the living room area that forked off to a hallway leading to a series of bedrooms.

Bryan had told Dennis he was safer upstairs, but he refused to listen.

He slid against the wall, trying to stay as calm as he could. His world collided when he heard Charlie screaming. He scrambled down the hallway, entering the bedroom he knew was hers. She wasn't inside. Was she with Dennis in his room?

He retraced his steps out into the hall and headed down to the next room, the door slightly open. He was almost afraid that whoever was there was standing in wait for someone to come in.

He heaved a breath and pushed it open, finding Charlie on the other side of the bed with Dennis, both their eyes focused on the far wall. That had to be where the intruder was standing, but he couldn't see at this vantage point. On the ground was another one of the Valor men, his face on the floor, his head facing away. He thought it was Leo. He was still, though he could tell he was breathing.

How was he going to get to this shooter without getting himself shot in the process? He wasn't sure, but he had to do something quickly before Dennis and Charlie took a bullet.

He would make a beeline for the bed and hope to get off a shot.

He dove forward, then rolled over, his arm steady and aimed at the target. He pulled the trigger, hitting the man wearing all black and a ski mask in the gut. He went down, clutching his belly.

Bryan sprinted to get the gun he'd dropped on the floor.

Once it was secured, he handed it to Dennis. "Watch him while I check Leo."

Bryan slowly turned his buddy over, finding blood soaking his side. His eyes fluttered open.

"Charlie, call 911."

She raced to the phone on the nightstand and called, her beautiful eyes now filled with tears.

Dammit. How had Beal and Emery found out they were here? There had to be a leak somewhere. But who was it? All their teams were vetted. He couldn't imagine any of them being a traitor for any amount of money.

Sirens in the distance had Bryan returning his attention to Leo. He lifted his shirt to see the wound, thankful that it probably didn't hit any vital organs.

"Someone is going to have to let the paramedics in."

"I'll go." Charlie ran from the room.

Where were Jake and Hank? Did they go AWOL? Sleep through the gunfire? It was strange that neither were here now that the shootout was over.

Two paramedics stepped into the room, and Bryan moved away, thinking of Kurt. He ran to where he'd seen him last, finding another EMT working on him. Time for him to locate the two missing men. They had to be here somewhere unless they were indeed working with the enemy.

He raced up to the second floor, opening doors, not finding them anywhere. Vince would be devastated if they had helped Beal find Dennis and Charlie. His men were his family. If they turned on their own, his boss would never be able to trust again.

He stepped down stairs again and searched the lower level, not finding them. They were gone, unless one of them was the man wearing the ski mask.

He went back to Dennis's room and was shocked. The EMTs had removed the mask, and lying on the floor was Jake. The guy shot his fellow ex-soldiers, but why? The whole thing made no sense.

He needed to call the boss and tell him, but this was going to be the hardest thing he'd ever had to do. Vincent was going to be devastated.

****

Charlie had recognized the man as one of the crew who they arrived with—part of Bryan's team. Her father would probably be dead right now had one of the others not stopped them by taking a bullet. She heard other shots before the gunmen found them. She had no idea if anyone else had been hurt. Thank God Bryan had showed up and got the jump on the shooter, or she and her dad would probably be dead. Again, he'd saved her life. He was more than just her hero. So much more. Hopefully, her father would be able to see that now.

Bryan stepped back into the room, his eyes glued to his colleague lying on the floor. The betrayal in his eyes was palpable. He was shocked, and so was she. Why had this man tried to kill them? Did he work for Beal? Or was this Sanderson's doing? Why would they send men with them who had no loyalty to the job? It made no sense. But then again, she had no idea what her father knew and how bad this all was.

Bryan came over to her, his arm going around her shoulder. “Are you okay?” Concern was clear in his eyes.

She pointed at the shooter. “I don’t understand.”

“You and me both, Charlie. I’ve known him since I started at Valor. I have no idea how Beal got him to go against his creed to do this. Vince will not take this well. Loyalty is everything to him. Come on. The police are going to want to question all of us. Let’s let them take him away and wait in the kitchen.”

Charlie took one last look at the man EMTs were working on, an officer standing by for security.

She allowed Bryan to lead her to the kitchen, everything suddenly feeling overwhelming to her. What would cause a man to betray his team? Did they find something to blackmail him with to get him to do this? She would never do anything to harm the people she worked with. They always had each other’s backs. What this man did went against everything she’d ever been taught.

“Can I get you some water?” Bryan’s question drew her out of her troubled thoughts.

“How about something stronger? Is there any gin?”

“Let me look. Do you want it straight up, or with a chaser?”

“A little tonic water would be nice.”

“I’ll see what I can do.” He entered the door off the kitchen, and returned a minute later with a bottle of high-end gin and some tonic water. “I think there are some limes in the fridge if you want a twist.”

She walked over to the refrigerator and pulled one out, then found a knife to slice it up. “You are going to join me, aren't you?"

Bryan frowned. "I'm not sure I should."

"After what just happened, we both need a drink, Bryan."

"All right, but just one for me." He poured gin in two tumblers and added the tonic.

Charlie slid the lime over the rim of the glasses, then squeezed the remaining juice into the drinks.

She lifted hers and took a large gulp and sighed. "Perfect."

He took a sip of his and nodded in agreement. At that moment, two officers stepped into the kitchen. "We've talked to everyone but you two. Can you tell me what happened, and don't leave anything out?"

By the time the police left, Charlie was working on her third drink and was starting to feel a bit loopy. She hadn't seen her father since she and Bryan left the bedroom. Where he was, she had no clue. He might have gone to talk to someone on the phone. She should go look for him, but she didn't want to, and then they'd probably argue about what he was keeping from her that almost got them killed. No. She'd rather stay with Bryan. He was so alluring. So damned sexy, and the alcohol was just making it harder to ignore that fact.

"Maybe you should go to bed, Charlie. Tomorrow is going to be a long day."

"Only if you come with me." Did that really come out of her mouth? She had never been this brazen with any man before, but she wanted Bryan with a burning passion. To hell with her pride, as long as he didn't turn her down.

"I don't think your father would like that. He seems to not like me all that much."

“Nonsense. What’s not to like? You just saved his life after all.”

He cleared his throat. “I still think he’d not be happy catching us together in bed.”

“If you don’t want to sleep with me, Bryan, just say so. Don’t use my father as an excuse.”

“It’s not that I don’t want to. I’ve thought about it many times since we’ve been together, but you are a client, Charlie, and Vince wouldn’t be happy with us mixing business with pleasure.”

“And your job is everything to you, right?”

“It’s pretty important, yes.”

Charlie placed her glass down onto the counter. “Good night, Bryan.”

“Charlie I—”

She raised a hand to stop him from saying anything else. “Is it okay to use your bedroom upstairs?”

“Of course. I’ll see you in the morning.”

Charlie headed for the stairs, angry that Bryan was more like her father than she’d first thought. The job was everything, and to hell with anything else.

Chapter 24

Bryan knew that Charlie was trying hard to hide her hurt and anger, but he knew he'd crushed her by saying no to her invitation. He would have loved to go with her, spend the whole night exploring her amazing body, but Dennis and Vince would have been livid. He might have also lost his job, and he liked what he did, no matter how much she had come to mean to him.

He walked out of the kitchen in search of what was left of their team. How one of their own men could do what they did was still plaguing him. He could never do that.

Hell, he wouldn't even sleep with Charlie, thinking it'd go against the team's rules. This guy completely betrayed them, actually shot two members of his own team to get to Dennis.

The whole thing was baffling on a major scale, and no matter how long he'd try to, he'd never understand why.

He found Hank standing by the open doors to the pool area. "Do you know where Dennis is?"

"He's in one of the downstairs bedrooms on his laptop."

"Can you tell me how Jake could have gone rogue against us?"

The man's eyes narrowed. "Your guess is as good as mine, Bryan. What the man did goes against anything we've ever been taught. I've known him for over two years. Had barbecues at his house. Hell, our wives are best friends. I have no idea what happened to make him turn on us. Oh, not sure if you heard or not but Leo and Kurt are recovering at the local hospital."

"That's a relief. Did anyone call Vince?"

"He's on his way here as we speak. We will all have to regroup once we can get in a room alone with him. I'm sure he is furious with himself for not coming on this trip. Maybe if he would have been here, perhaps Jake wouldn't have attempted this."

"We can't let him blame himself. The man still is grieving Bolton's death."

"Those two were thick as thieves. Vince will never get over his loss."

"Where were you when this all went down? Kurt went down first and then Leo."

"In the pool. I couldn't sleep after we all went in the for the night. I thought maybe a few laps would help. If I'd been in the house, Jake might not have done what he did. Vince was like a dad to him, but I was like a brother. In the morning, after our powwow with Vince, I'm going to the hospital to find out why he'd do something like this. I hope he'll tell me the truth."

"Do you think Vince will fill us in on why they want Dennis dead? Being left in the dark is frustrating, especially for his daughter."

Hank shrugged. "I don't know. We've done a few assignments where we didn't know the nuts and bolts of the job going in. This is probably your first. I noticed that you and Dennis's daughter seem pretty close. Be careful there, at least until the job is concluded. Once it's complete and we are onto another assignment, I wouldn't think Vince would have any reservations about you two dating. Her father, on the other hand…"

"Yeah, the congressman doesn't seem to care for me."

"Put yourself in his shoes, Bryan. You are all about your job. His daughter would always be second to that."

"How do you make it work with your wife?"

Hank smiled. "Candace has a job she also loves, and we have a three-year-old that keeps us both grounded. As long as you both know going in what to expect, then it can work."

Charlie loved her job. Maybe she wouldn't want him to give up anything to be with her. But that was something they'd have to talk about once this mission was over. They were in the middle of a shitstorm right now, and thinking about anything else had to wait.

****

Charlie rolled over, sunlight through the window making her squint her eyes. Her head hurt. Must be from the alcohol she had. One too many from the way her head felt.

Her conversation with Bryan last night came flooding back. She had propositioned him, and he'd turned her down. Talk about embarrassing. She wasn't going to be able to face him today. Throwing yourself at a man was so pathetic, no matter how many drinks she'd had.

She shoved the covers aside and walked into the bathroom. Her bags were downstairs, but she could shower and put something of Bryan's on. One of his tees and boxers until she could change into her own clothes. Under the spray, she used the products that were there, the shampoo and conditioner of high quality and smelled of wildflowers.

The body wash was similar, and when she was rinsed off, she sighed, feeling so much better.

She stepped out onto the mat and grabbed a towel to dry off. Then she wrapped another around her wet hair and went to go through Bryan's duffel. She found a tee and boxers, slipped into them and started drying her hair, a knock on the door had her wondering if it was Bryan. She really wasn't ready to face him yet. But she might not have a choice.

"Charlie, are you up?" her father asked.

She went to open the door.

"I'm getting ready to head over to Capitol Hill. I thought I should talk to you before I leave."

She moved away for him to step inside the room.

"The ethics committee is meeting today to question me. Apparently, it's going to be live. I'm planning to reveal things that need to come out. You need to watch. This is why Beal kidnapped you and tried to kill us last night. I should have gone to the media weeks ago. You wouldn't have been put in peril. I will never forgive myself for that. Please stay in the house. Bryan will be here to protect you, just in case they try for a last-ditch effort to stop me from telling the truth. Once it's revealed, there will be chaos in the halls of Congress—people will be arrested. I'll try to get back here as soon as I can. Then we will go back to Colorado until the smoke clears."

"But can't you tell me now?"

"It's best that you learn it when everyone else does."

Charlie watched her father leave, his shoulders staunch. What he knew was horrible, and it was hard for him to do what he was about to do. She knew that. But once today was over, she and her father could go back to their lives as it was before.

Suddenly, that didn't sit well with her. This ordeal had changed her. She didn't want what she had before. Yes, she loved her job, but she wanted more now. She wanted Bryan, but it was clear he didn't feel the same. That caused tears to well in her eyes. But somehow, she was going to have to get over him. She didn't have a choice.

Charlie walked back to the bathroom to finish drying her hair. She was determined to get through the day with Bryan. Then, after her father returned, they'd go their own way. Maybe with enough time, she would think fond thoughts of her and Bryan's time together. Hopefully, it wouldn't take long because the two could run into each other since they both lived in Winding Creek, and she didn't want to be sad every time that happened.

When she finished with her hair, she left his room to go to the bedroom where her bag was, so she could get dressed. She would return Bryan's clothes to his bag after she did.

She managed to make it to the bedroom without running into anyone. Charlie was thankful for that.

When she changed into her own clothes, she refolded his and retraced her steps, again hoping not to run into Bryan. She was still trying to figure out what to say. She needed to appear unfazed about his actions from last night. He didn't need to know how much they'd hurt her. Somehow, that would just make things worse.

Upstairs in his room, she tucked his clothes back in his duffel, then left again. She could really use a cup of coffee. She hoped Bryan wasn't in the kitchen.

She had to find a device to watch the congressional hearings on. Surely this place had a TV, or ten.

On the way to the kitchen, she ran into the only other man they'd arrived with. He was coming in the door.

Who was going to the halls of Congress with her father? She hated the idea of him being there alone.

"Hello," she said to him, not sure what else to say.

"Hey. Do you know where Bryan is?"

"I've only been up a while. I haven't seen him this morning. I was heading into the kitchen. He might be there."

He gave her a slight smile, "I'll follow you."

Charlie continued toward the kitchen, feeling his eyes on her back. The man was handsome, but not nearly as much as Bryan, and after last night, she wasn't sure if she could even trust him.

She swung the kitchen door open and hesitated for a moment when she saw Bryan sitting at the table, a large mug of steaming coffee in front of him.

He saw her and sat up straight. "Hank. How are Kurt and Leo doing?" Bryan asked his colleague.

"They are doing fine. Jake is still in intensive care, and only family is allowed to see him. So, I didn't get to find out anything. Leo and Kurt were shocked to learn it was Jake who shot them. They had no clue who or how someone got to him. Though, Jake did take a call and walked off while talking when we were all outside last night. We need to get our hands on his phone and find out who made that call."

Charlie walked over to get a cup of coffee. She was going to stay out of the conversation, since she had nothing to contribute. Let them talk. That way she could avoid having any discussion now. She was going to go

find a TV and see if it had CSPAN, probably the only station that would carry the hearing.

She left the kitchen. There had to be a den or study that had a television, or a device she could watch her father on. If not, she'd have to wait for him to get back to find out what all this was about—and she didn't have the patience for that.

Chapter 25

Bryan saw Charlie leave the room and knew she was trying to avoid him. Maybe that was for the best. Since Vince arrived, he had been on point—the job that he was hired to do. His boss had a way of making that more important than anything while he was around.

Vincent and two other Valor employees he'd brought with him had left with Dennis, determined that nothing else happened before the hearing at nine O'clock. Jake's betrayal had crushed Vince, and he'd left angry with the world. But anger only fueled the man. He would make sure Dennis stayed safe.

"At the hospital, I asked if I could get Jake's things," Hank said, drawing Bryan back to the man. "But his phone wasn't there. I'm thinking he may have dropped it when he went down. Can you show me which room they were in?"

"Sure." Bryan rose, exited the kitchen and walked down the hallway to the bedroom, blood splotched on the carpet.

He pointed to where he'd shot Jake. "That's where he was. The other is Leo's blood."

Hank started to look around, leaning down to see under the dresser nearby. "There it is."

He squatted to get the phone and then stood again, trying to open the phone. "It's password-protected."

"You know him better than me. He's married, right?

Maybe his wife's name? Her birthday? His birthday?"

He punched something in and cursed when it didn't work. Not his wife's name.

He tried again with the same results. Dammit. What could it be? Wait a minute.

He tried again, then smiled and showed Bryan that it worked.

"What was it?"

"Bolton."

"He uses Valor and then betrays us. I don't get it."

"We may never know why, Bryan, but here is that number from last night. Should we call and see who answers?"

"Yes. Maybe pretend to be Jake. You two have similar voices. Perhaps they won't catch it right away."

He punched redial and waited.

Bryan held his breath. Whoever was on the other end was in on this attempted murder.

"It's about fucking time you got back to me," a man said, clearly angry. "Is the job done?"

"Yeah." Hank glanced at Bryan.

"Good. We will release your wife the minute we have confirmation."

Bryan's eyes widened. No wonder Jake had done what he had. They'd used his wife as leverage to get him to shoot Dennis. That meant that Jake's wife was in danger the minute they learned that Dennis was testifying this morning. Sterling needed to trace this number and find out where it was coming from. Bryan stepped away and called him, telling him to trace the number and get a location. Then, send some men to rescue Jake's wife.

That done, he walked back in, thinking that man's

voice sounded familiar, but it wasn't Beal. *Wait.* Was it Emery's assistant? The man he talked to that first day on this job. He'd almost bet money on it. That meant Sanderson was involved in this whole sorted mess, too. What was he and Beal's connection? There had to be something. Maybe Sterling could find out what.

He'd call him back and see. If he couldn't work on that, then he'd go in search of Charlie. Yes, she was mad at him, but she was his responsibility until Dennis returned. If she wanted that or not.

He took out his phone, found Sterling and pressed call.

"We have someone on the way to rescue Jake's wife. Did you need something else?"

"I want you to look for a connection between Nathan Beal and Sanderson Emery."

"That's easy. They are both on the board of WonderCo, a charitable foundation that ships lifesaving supplies around the world."

Didn't Beal's brother deal in shipping containers? What lifesaving supplies were these men handling? Were they what they say they were, or something else altogether? "Can you find out who else is on that board?"

"Sure thing. Give me an hour."

"Thanks, Sterling."

Bryan ended the call. His head was now spinning. What was worth killing over? Drugs? Guns? Human trafficking? Maybe all of the above?

Was this what Dennis had been keeping under wraps?

Bryan glanced at the time. The hearing would be starting soon. Would Dennis reveal whatever these two men were involved in today? Or did he have something

else to share? He'd just have to wait and see.

****

Charlie sat down on the sofa and turned on the large screen TV. The hearing was only minutes away, and she needed to find a station that was planning to cover it. When she found CSPAN, Bryan stepped into the room and sat in a chair. Just being near him caused her skin to prickle, her heart to pick up pace. She needed to stay focused on the TV to keep her face from flushing.

People started filing into the room, the committee chair taking the seat at the middle on the top row. When the congressmen were all seated, Charlie's father, his chief of staff, and her father's attorney, entered through doors at the back of the room and sat at the table, three microphones stationed in front of them. Vincent and three other men were sitting in chairs behind them. Were they there to protect her father? Charlie wasn't sure, but she was glad they were there just in case.

The committee chair, Henry Alderman, introduced them to the audience, then turned his full attention on her father. "Congressman Reed, you have a prepared statement."

"I do, Mr. Alderman."

"Go ahead then. You have our full attention."

"Thank you. First, I want to thank the committee for giving me a chance to refute the charges they've laid against me. The pictures that were shown earlier, the ones that have been publicized, are fake. We know that this is easily done with our technology today. I've never met the woman in the pictures, though she has sent me emails with a sonogram of a fetus, not mine, since I have never met her. This was an elaborate ruse to discredit me because of something I've learned about some powerful people on Capitol Hill and beyond. If I may. I've invited someone to speak on this subject."

The chairs gavel started to bang. "This is highly irregular, Congressman. We were not told beforehand that you were going to have guest speakers."

"I'm sorry about that, but we were only able to confirm the appearance three hours ago. Like I said, they will be able to clear up all of this."

"Can you tell me who this mystery speaker is?"

"Like I said, they are waiting outside the room. You will see as soon as they enter."

Charlie turned to Bryan, who was glued to the TV. "Do you know who the person is?"

He shook his head. "No idea."

Minutes seemed to tick by as the committee chair talked to a few of the other members, then turned their attention back to her father. "We will allow your guest to speak."

"Thank you, Mr. Alderman." He signaled to a man sitting in the back, who rose and walked to the door.

He waved for the person on the other side to come in. The room became electrified. The door came open and in walked a stunning, olive-skinned, voluptuous beauty dressed in a black suit.

"Do you know who she is?" Charlie asked Bryan.

"I don't. I think we are about to find out."

The quiet in the room changed to complete mayhem. Some of those people, including a few of the committee members, clearly knew who she was and were not happy to see her—not one bit.

Her father's chief of staff had moved to the front row to make room for her to take a seat.

The chairman didn't seem to know who she was and

asked her to state her name and what she wanted to tell the committee.

Charlie watched as they panned out around the room, four of the members looking as if they were about to lose their lunch. Something bothered them, but what?

"I want to thank you, Chairman, for allowing me to speak to the committee today. My name is Andria Garcia. I work in Congressman Sebert's office as an aide. I've worked there for just over five months. Two and a half months into my tenure, I was asked by Mr. Sebert to join a few of the team to attend a party at another of the congressmen's homes. I tried to say no, but he insisted. I really didn't feel like I had a choice. Twenty-five minutes after arriving, I started to feel woozy. I tried to leave but was denied. Congressman Sebert had given me a glass of wine, one I had only taken a few sips from, but that's when I realized that he had put something in the drink. The room started to spin, and the congressman ushered me into another room where there were people in all types of undress, doing things I'd only seen on TV. I tried to get away, but three other men came over and dragged me farther into the room. I don't remember much after that, though I know I was sexually assaulted. I woke up in the back of a van, two other women were there as well. They had no idea where we were. When someone finally came to open the door, I saw rows of shipping containers. All I could think of was they were going to put us in one and ship us somewhere. I managed to kick the man hard enough to get away, and I ran until I could call my friend, who came and took me to the hospital. I was examined, and a rape kit was done. One thing I do remember about that night was those three men. They are in this room right now."

The room erupted in angry voices.

The committee chair seemed to find his tongue and asked, "Who are those three men, Ms. Garcia?"

"Congressman Jacks, Vertice, and Melbourne."

"I object. This is all lies," Congressman Jacks yelled.

"No, it's not," her father said. "We have it all on video. All but the part where you tried to sex traffic Ms. Garcia. You should never trust anyone at these sex parties you sickos throw on the weekends. Someone came forward with the evidence. Also, we found the connection between at least twelve congressmen and senators who get a kickback from Nathan Beal and his brother, who are partnered with Sanderson Emery in the human trafficking business. And yes, I have evidence of that as well. This is why my daughter was kidnapped last week, and I was almost murdered last night."

Chapter 26

Bryan was still in shock after watching the hearing. Televised for the world to see. He couldn't believe there were twelve of their representatives involved in this atrocity. Would they resign or have to be expelled? That was something they'd have to see in the coming days. If they were smart, they'd get out quickly, before every sordid detail came out. Then they'd have their faces plastered from here to Timbuktu. Bryan felt sorry for the men's families. They, too, would have to pay the price for the greed of their family members.

Bryan walked to the kitchen. Dennis would be there soon to collect his daughter, and then he'd probably never see her again. That should have made him relieved, but it didn't. For whatever reason, he'd come to enjoy her company, even though most of the time they were trying to stay alive. Maybe he missed the adrenaline rush the military gave him, and that's why he'd felt alive with her?

Or perhaps it was something else. Like he had grown fond of her. Yes, the attraction was clear, but there was more. Charlie was special. She brought out the nurturing side in him, a part he never knew existed until now.

He needed a drink even though it wasn't five yet. He had to admit, he'd enjoyed the gin and tonic that Charlie had the night before—too many since they'd made her proposition him. He still felt bad saying no to that invitation. Most would have jumped at it, but Vince was already in a bad place because of Jake. The man didn't need Bryan to disappoint him further. No matter how much he might have wanted to sleep with Charlie.

Bryan quickly fixed himself a drink and went out to the patio. It was beautiful here. Whoever owned this home was lucky indeed. The place was like paradise.

He sat in a chaise lounge and took a long sip of his drink, squeezing his eyes closed, enjoying the sun hitting his face. It was the perfect setting, perfect day, except it would be his last with Charlie.

And she was going to leave angry with him. That was the hardest part. But it was for the best. *Why doesn't it feel like the best?*

He should finish his drink, then go up and pack his stuff. He was sure they were expected to clear out as soon as Dennis and Vince returned. Hell, the jet was probably already fueled and ready to go back to Colorado—Bolton Valor onto their next mission. With three of their men in the hospital.

Bryan downed the rest of his drink. He almost wished he'd never met Charlie now. For some reason, the idea of saying goodbye hurt.

He rose and walked back to the kitchen to rinse his glass and then placed it into the dishwasher. Before they left, they'd need to run it.

He took the stairs to the room he'd been given and gathered up his belongings, stuffing them into his duffel bag. The sooner they got out of there, the sooner he'd get over Charlie and move on with his life.

A knock startled him out of his troubled thoughts.

Standing in the doorway was Charlie, her too, not

looking happy.

"Is your dad back?"

She shook her head. "Not yet. I just wanted to thank you for everything you did for me, Bryan. You saved my life twice. I can never repay that."

"My job was to find you and keep you safe. I'm glad I was able to do that." The tightening in his chest became almost painful. He was seriously going to miss seeing her, talking to her, just breathing the air she did. How had she become so important to him in such a short time? Especially when it was so uncharacteristic of him to feel anything for anyone.

She gave him a small smile. "Still, I wanted to get a chance to thank you again before my father arrives. I'm sure this will be the last chance for us to be alone before we leave."

The last chance for them to be alone hit him hard. He wanted to tell her she was more than just an assignment. So much more. But Vince's face kept him from doing so. She was still *the job.* Until she wasn't, he couldn't say what he wanted to. "I'm glad everything turned out okay, Charlie. That you and your father will go on with your lives as usual."

The smile on her face vanished, in its place was hurt. *Shit.* Whatever he said had not been taken the way he'd meant it. Dammit. He wasn't good at sentiment—never had been. His upbringing was at the core. That and his ADHD had his brain running too fast for his mouth. In the service, it kept him on his toes. In real-life situations, it was a disaster.

Dennis calling her name gave him the reprieve he needed. Thank God.

She turned and left, taking a part of his heart with

her. Of course, she'd never know that now. His words had hurt her, and he doubted she'd go out of her way to call once they were back in Winding Creek and the assignment had ended. This was goodbye forever for her.

****

Charlie stepped off the plane, intending not to look back. Bryan had made his intentions clear. The gig was up, and he was going his merry way. She needed to get that through her head now—this had been a mission and nothing more to him. To her, it was something different altogether. She'd fallen hard, and she wasn't stupid enough to tell him that. Who would be a glutton for punishment like that or in their right mind to tell the truth when it was clear he didn't feel the same?

A limo was waiting for her and her father, along with a black SUV that would take the Valor men back to their place of business. This was the end of the road. She'd probably never see any of them again. That was probably for the best.

"Are you okay?" her father asked once they were in the car and on their way home.

"Why wouldn't I be?"

"You've been awful quiet since we left DC."

"Just trying to unwind everything. How long did you know what was going on with this sex trafficking stuff?"

"Too long for my sanity."

"How did Nathan find out about you knowing?"

"That was my fault. I didn't know he was involved until a month ago. Everything started to unravel with his brother's shipping company being implicated. Them using their containers to traffic these men and women, some only teenagers. When Sanderson's name came up in all this and you were supposedly dating him, that's when things got hairy. I wanted to talk to you about all of this, but I didn't want to tip my hand before everything was in place to catch all involved. Especially some of my colleagues who could be shielded by their positions. But I should have protected you first and foremost. I will never forgive myself for letting them kidnap you."

"Will all of them be arrested?"

"I hope so, Charlie, but you know that money and power can sometimes be enough to get people off, no matter how horrendous the crimes are."

Charlie had seen how many abusers were given slaps on the hand in the court system. That had jaded her to justice, but this surely would be bad enough for these representatives to at least lose their seats by the voters of their states. If not, there was no longer a rule of law. Or morality in this country.

Once arriving at her father's house, she went off to her room, not in the right frame of mind to spend any more time chatting with her father. She needed to think about the last week and how she was going to move forward with her life. Suddenly, everything felt different. Her world was no longer the same. Bryan had changed everything. Too bad she hadn't changed his life.

She was going to go take a long, hot shower and hope it helped to relieve all this angst not being with him had created. Even the time spent in the panic room with him was better than not being with him. How had these days with Bryan changed her whole life? Why was her chest hurting now? Tears filled her eyes, and she allowed herself to cry as she undressed and stepped into the shower, the spray mingling with her tears. Maybe this was just her decompressing from the stress of running for her life. Perhaps it had nothing to do with Bryan.

Images of him came flooding back, the feel of his lips on hers causing her to suck in a ragged breath. Nope. This was not her coming to terms with her ordeal. This was her wanting him like she had never wanted anyone before, and there wasn't a damn thing she could do to change that. She was in love for the first time in her life and it had to be with someone who didn't feel the same.

Chapter 27

It had been a week since Bryan had watched Charlie disappear into the limo, and even their new assignment hadn't helped to keep his mind off missing her with every breath he took. He didn't understand this feeling of grief—like someone had died and there was no escape from the pain. Everywhere he looked, he saw her face. It was driving him crazy.

"Did you hear what I said, Bryan?" Sterling said over the phone line. *Nope. Not a damned word. Shit.* If he didn't pull himself together, he was going to lose his job.

"Sorry, Sterling. Can you repeat that?"

"I said, Marvin Dills was not on that video conference call, according to the other members. He has no alibi for that afternoon."

"And you are sure about that?"

"Yes. Is there anything else you need? Maybe a day or two off, perhaps?"

Bryan was confused by Sterling's suggestion. "No. Why would I need time off?"

"I just think something has you distracted. At least take the night off. There isn't anything else you can do until morning anyway."

Sterling was right. He needed to get some sleep—another thing that had been troubling him since he left Charlie's side. Every time he closed his eyes, she was there with that look of sadness on her face that he'd caused. He was never going to forgive himself for that. Not ever.

"You're right, Sterling. I'm going to head home, and we'll start in the morning early."

"I'll talk to you then."

Bryan turned his car around and headed for home, only to have his navigation reboot to show Charlie's place of work. What the hell? It had never done this before. So why now? Was someone trying to tell him something? It sure seemed like it. Maybe he'd bumped something.

Would she be there anyway? After her ordeal, she might have taken time off to spend with her father, though Dennis had been in DC the past two days with congressional hearings on the representatives who were holding out to keep their jobs, even with proof of their guilt. Took a lot of balls to try to stay the course when you were as dirty as they were. They would have been better off going quietly. Trafficking was such a disgusting thing, and yet the men elected to protect people from this were making money from it. How much lower could a public official go?

He stared at the screen, Charlie's beautiful face causing him to suck in a ragged breath. Perhaps she wouldn't be so unhappy to see him if he did show up. But what if she was? How would he be able to deal with that?

Fuck it. He missed her, and he wanted to see her, if only for a moment or two.

He turned onto the road, headed her way, trying to figure out what he was going to say. Should he come right out and tell her they could be together now that he was no longer protecting her? How would she take that? He didn't know, and by the time he reached her place of work, he'd managed to question if she'd want to see him or not.

Bryan sat in his SUV, running all these scenarios through his brain, all ending with her saying go away—that she never wanted to see him again.

No. This was stupid. He had to man up and find out one way or the other. If he didn't, he'd never know, and he'd always wonder. That would be worse than her saying she hated him and to go away forever.

Here goes nothing.

He popped the door open and walked up the sidewalk, his insides shaking. *Buck up. You are an ex-Army ranger, for God's sakes. Are you going to let a tiny slip of a woman scare the pants off you?*

Bryan opened the door, determined to make Charlie see that they were meant to be together, even if he had to throw her over his shoulder and carry her to the panic room for a week to do so.

****

Charlie heard her name being called to the front over the intercom and wondered why. Maybe they had a new client for her.

She glanced at the time in the corner of her computer screen and saw that it was almost closing time. Unfortunately, abuse had no time frame. She'd learned that the first week on the job. Perhaps this was what she needed. A new client to keep her mind off Bryan for at least a few hours. He'd been stuck there like an old movie reel slipping in a projector. Her heart had been breaking since she returned to her condo after Nathan Beal, his brother, and her fake boyfriend had been arrested for kidnapping—only the first of their charges. More would come. Though, they had to prove that Sanderson was involved and with all his money, that could be hard to do.

Eight of her father's colleagues had resigned, and they were still waiting on the others who seemed to think they could weather this storm. Hopefully, with enough pressure, they would see there was no way to keep their seats.

Charlie rose from her chair and headed for the front, inwardly praying this case wasn't as bad as the last one she'd worked.

In the years she had been there, she had seen horrible abuse by the men who claimed to love their wives, girlfriends, and children. That couldn't have been any further from the truth.

When she reached the receptionist's area, her heart literally stopped. Byran stood off to the side, and he looked too good to be true. Had she conjured him up by thinking of him? Or was he really here to see her?

She swallowed hard, her mouth becoming clogged with emotion. At that moment, she knew something for sure. She had strong feelings for this man, and all it had taken was for them to spend a few short days together. How would she feel if they had time to get to know one another without having to try to stay alive? Doing silly, mundane things that normal people did?

"Hello," he said when she didn't say anything.

"Hi." Why did her brain have a hard time forming words? He'd caused every coherent thought to leave her.

"Can I speak to you outside?"

"Okay."

He allowed her to lead the way, feeling his eyes on

her back, only making it harder for her to think straight.

Why had he come?

Out the door, she took a long, labored breath, hoping it'd help clear her head. Otherwise, she doubted she'd be able to form a sentence.

"I'm sorry that I waited a week to talk to you, Charlie. I knew you'd need time with your father."

Charlie inhaled, not knowing how to respond or if he even wanted her to.

Seconds ticked by, him looking at her intently, to the point that it caused beads of sweat to roll down her back. Now, she was going to have to say something. "Why are you here, Bryan?"

He squeezed his eyes closed. He was struggling with what he wanted to say, too. She could see that. "I've had days to think about our time together, and I came to realize that I have feelings for you."

Wasn't this what she wanted to hear—that he felt something too? But feelings weren't enough when they we so different. Hadn't she said she'd never date or marry a military man? *My God.* Bryan was the epitome of that for sure. The job was everything to him. Could she live with that? Being second to his career? She wasn't sure. Hadn't she watched her own mother have trouble watching her dad leave for yet another tour?

Though, Bryan was no longer serving in the armed forces. But she saw that he couldn't cross a line with her, even though she knew he wanted to. That meant his job was all-encompassing, and she would always take a back seat to whatever he was working on.

He shifted from one foot to the other, drawing her back to him. It had been hard for him to tell her what he just had. She had to give him props for that. "I was hurt when you rejected me in DC, Bryan. I feel like I will never be as important as your next mission. I watched my own mother suffer over this. I'm not sure if I'm willing or able to do it like she did."

"I get it, Charlie. I've been all about the job for so many years that it's hard to change, but I am willing to try for you." The emotion in his voice was clear. He meant what he was saying. So, why not see where the two could go? Maybe choosing him would be worth it. At least with him by her side, she'd never have to worry about being in danger. The man would always save her. When he found her on that mountain, she was a stranger to him, and yet he risked his own life to keep her safe. Imagine if they were a couple, she'd never have to worry about being kidnapped again. But was that worth risking her heart? She guessed there was only one way to find out.

"Take me to dinner and we'll see where that goes."

Charlie had never seen Bryan smile, a real one that caused her breath to catch in her chest. For some reason, that smile made her look forward to what was to come—to hell with everything else.

A word about the author...

Jerri Drennen is an author of romantic suspense as well as paranormal and contemporary romance. Growing up on a farm in a tiny town in Minnesota was where she started reading romance and learned how to make up stories in her head. After meeting her husband, she moved to his hometown in Missouri where she now live with one of their four children. Her kids call her the crazy cat lady.

Thank you for purchasing
this publication of The Wild Rose Press, Inc.

For questions or more information
contact us at
info@thewildrosepress.com.

The Wild Rose Press, Inc.
www.thewildrosepress.com